STORM OF SIN

PATRICIA D. EDDY

ONE

Zoe

Have you ever had a day so bizarre, you spend every waking moment convinced someone is going to jump out from around a corner and yell *"Punked"*?

Well, it's happening. To me. Right now.

In the past twenty-four hours, I've gone from the laughing stock of the San Francisco Police Department, constantly ridiculed for my insistence there were supernatural forces at work in the City by the Bay, to the newest junior agent at the Bureau of the Occult and the Other.

B.O.O. for short.

Yes. Really. Our name is BOO.

Three Weeks Ago

Zoe

The parking lot feels empty, and the fog is already starting to give the world a soft, white glow. The swelling under my right eye doesn't help. The stench of the scumbag I arrested this morning still clings to me, even after two showers and changing into the backup shirt I keep in my locker.

The guy reeked of sweat and cheap liquor, and when I found him trying to break in to a bunker out at the abandoned Hunter's Point Naval Shipyard, he got the best of me and landed a hard punch just south of my eye.

The detective in charge—Randall—sent me out with no backup, then had the gall to keep me out of the interrogation room while he questioned the guy. The rash of vandalism and break-ins at abandoned buildings across the city has been a thorn in the department's side for weeks, but the perp gave DIC Randall nothing. Just two words. Over and over again.

His eyes. His eyes. His eyes.

I wish I'd been able to talk myself into the room. But my partner, Temple, called in sick three days ago, and apparently, I'm "a loose cannon" because *once*, I made the mistake of telling Detective Randall that my grandmother taught me to respect the world of the *Other*.

Well, there was also that one time I accused a sex worker of being a shifter. But I saw *scales* ripple over the back of her neck when I arrested her. What else could she have been?

Gingerly, I touch the swelling along my cheek and let the wind coming off the San Francisco Bay ruffle my hair. I love this city. Even when it's cold and foggy and damp. My earliest memory is seeing the bay with my grandmother. I can still feel her hand on my shoulder like it was yesterday.

"One day, Zoe, you'll understand how special you are. This city, this view...treasure it. Here, you'll do great things. I know it."

I miss Nana so very much. I don't remember my parents, and though I never put stock in her assertion that I was sculpted by the angels, that I was her little miracle, the world of the Other? That's real. It has to be. Nana knew things before they happened, and when she cried, it always seemed to rain.

Retrieving my keys from my jacket pocket, I skid on some wet leaves a few steps from my car. Shit. I need another shower, a glass of wine, and an ice pack for my cheek. I'm so tired, I'm losing my edge.

A soft footfall registers a second too late. Before I can turn, something hard jabs me in the back, and cold fingers wrap around my throat.

"Not a sound, Zoe."

"Temple?" I whisper. "What are you doing...?"

My partner tightens his grip, and I fall silent.

"Unlock the car, get in the passenger side, and cuff yourself to the door handle."

My hand shakes as I fumble with the key fob. Temple sounds strange. His voice is hard and cold, so very different from the kind, jovial, teddy bear with an easy smile I've come to know and trust since being promoted to detective six months ago.

"This isn't you, Temple. Put down the gun and let's talk." His fingers tighten over my windpipe, making it hard to swallow, but he hasn't cut off my air. Yet.

The pressure of the pistol eases, but a moment later, the barrel slams into the back of my skull and I fall against the car, my keys jingling as they hit the ground.

"Pick them up. Now."

At least he doesn't have me by the throat anymore. But I'm dizzy, and pinpricks of light dot my vision. Nodding is a mistake, and my knees wobble. He grabs my right arm and twists it behind me, sending pain radiating from my shoulder to my fingertips.

Why didn't I leave when my shift was over? Two hours ago, there'd have been half a dozen other cops headed out with me, and I wouldn't be in a deserted parking lot alone. Or about to be kidnapped by the one man I should be able to trust more than anyone else in the world.

My service weapon is under my jacket, but with his hold on my wrist, I can't get to it.

"Temple, please," I whimper. "You're hurting me."

"Keys. Now."

Forcing me down, he keeps the gun pressed to my back, and I snag the fob and unlock my car.

It hurts even more when he pulls me up, and I curl my fingers around the door handle.

"Put down the gun!" a man shouts from across the parking lot. "Hands in the air."

The sharp pressure of the barrel shifts, and I ram my left elbow into Temple's gut, then stomp on his instep with all the strength I can muster.

A loud *crack* registers before my ears start to ring, and something warm and wet makes my shirt stick to my side.

Temple grunts as he doubles over, giving me a split second to jerk my wrist from his hold and pull my gun.

The shouts from my fellow officers are muffled, and the world seems to move in slow motion as I draw down on my partner. His eyes are glazed over, his mouth slack, but his gun is still trained on me.

"Temple! Listen!" My voice isn't steady, and I brace myself against the car so I won't fall. "It's Zoe. We're partners. *Friends*. Don't do this!"

A dozen uniforms and half as many detectives surround us, but Temple doesn't flinch, doesn't react at all.

When I meet his gaze, something unnatural slithers along my spine. It's like his personality, his very *soul* is gone, and all that's left is desperation.

"I never would have made detective without you. You're a good man." Fire burns through my side, and a quick glance has me stifling a whimper. My light green shirt is stained red with my blood, and the world tilts. He *shot* me. My own partner.

Temple blinks, hard, then focuses on my Smith & Wesson. "Do it," he says as a tear rolls down his cheek. "Can't fight...*him* any longer."

"Who?" The burning pain in my side is getting worse, and the gun wobbles. "Temple? Tell me..."

"You're...special, Zoe. Don't...tell anyone..." His eyes cloud over. "Run."

I only make it a single step when the crack of his .45 deafens me, and the bullet rips through my passenger window. I don't think. Training takes over, and I return fire. My ass hits the pavement, with Temple falling an arm's reach away.

Blood spurts from his neck, and he gurgles quietly as footsteps pound towards me.

"Zoe! Detective Dawes!" My sergeant kneels next to me and presses his hands to my side. "Stay with me. That's an order."

Sergeant Perkins isn't someone you mess with, even when you're about to pass out, and I clutch his arm. "Temple..."

Sirens blare in the distance, and I fight to hang on. We're surrounded now. Two uniforms drag Temple away, and every other officer on duty takes position in a solid blue wall around me and Perkins.

I can't see anymore, and Perkins' voice sounds like it's coming from miles away. "He's gone, Zoe. Whatever made him do this...we're going to get to the bottom of it."

TWO

Zoe

Pushing through the door of the Red Light Diner on Grand, I stifle a wince as I remove my sunglasses. Macie, the way-too-perky server on the breakfast shift, arches a brow, and I slink into a booth.

"What'll it be?" she asks, a weariness to her voice that I hear all too often.

"Tomato juice, heavy on the tabasco. And a glass of water," I say as I pull out a packet of Alka-Seltzer.

"So, the usual, then."

"Cut me some slack, Macie. You know I'm going through some shit." I close my eyes, the sandpaper that's taken residence on the inside of my lids scratching like a bitch. My own fault. I've fallen into a bottle more nights than not since I fired the shot that killed my partner.

"That's what I've *been* doing. No more," she says sharply. "Temple would be so disappointed in you."

That hurts. No. It threatens to destroy me. Temple was the only person in my life I could count on. Or so I thought. Dropping my head into my hands, I watch Macie's sensible black shoes shuffle away. A minute later, a glass lands on the table in front of me with a solid thunk. Then Macie rips open the Alka-Seltzer packet and the tablets plop into the water with a low fizz.

I peer up at her, my bloodshot eyes struggling to focus after yet another sleepless night. And those four shots of Jack. "Thanks."

"I'm not doing it for you," Macie says, her voice softening. "Temple was my friend too."

More than that. After three years of flirting, they'd finally gone out for a drink two days before Temple called in sick.

"I'm sorry." It's all I have. All I can muster, but I feel it down to my toes. And in my scar. That damn two-inch line of raised, reddish tissue from the operation to remove the bullet hurts like hell every time I take a deep breath. According to my doctor, I've healed perfectly, so the pain is psychosomatic. Doesn't make it hurt any less.

"You want breakfast?" Macie asks as she pulls out her order pad.

After the first sip of Alka-Seltzer, I clear my throat. "Denver Omelet. Extra—"

"Tabasco. I know." She reaches over and squeezes my shoulder. "One day at a time, Zoe. And maybe...try a night that ends with tea rather than whiskey?"

"Yeah. I know."

She heads for the kitchen to put my order in, and I sink back against the vinyl. In an hour, I'll be sitting at my desk, answering tip line calls. Sergeant Perkins won't let me back in the field until I can pass my psych eval, and after I told the doctor it was like Temple had been possessed, she tried to put me on antipsychotics. And told Perkins I was off balance.

So much for doctor-patient confidentiality.

My phone vibrates in my hip pocket as Macie drops off the omelet.

Unknown number.

I jab the screen and hold the phone away from my ear. Loud noises? Not so good at this point. "Who is this?"

"Detective Dawes? This is Lieutenant Grayson Eve with the San Francisco division of the Bureau of the Occult and the Other." The official-sounding female voice enunciates each syllable perfectly, but it takes my sluggish brain a moment to process her words.

"The what?"

"The Bureau of the Occult and the Other. We work the cases in the city that fall...*outside* the purview of civilian law enforcement."

"Outside?" Shit. I sound like an idiot.

"The paranormal, Detective Dawes. I don't think I need to explain further, do I?"

Straightening, ignoring the painful twinge in my side, I forget all about the omelet in front of me. "No. Sir. Ma'am. What...um... Why are you calling me?"

"I've read through your files."

"Files? I have...files? From where?" Darting a glance at Macie, I force a smile and wave her off as she starts to approach. Wherever this conversation is going...it needs to be private.

"SFPD, FBI, NSA... Everyone has been watching you for a while now, Dawes."

"Watching? Shit. I sound like a broken record. I'm sorry, but—"

"But you're hung over." The judgement is heavy in her words, and I look around wildly, searching for someone. Anyone who might be showing an unusual interest in me. Spying on me.

"Zoe, you're highly intelligent, curious, and, dare I say, aggressive. In your time with the SFPD, you've pissed off three separate commanders at three separate precincts because you've shown them up within six weeks of being assigned to their squads. Your instincts are spot on, and you know—*know*—without a doubt, that there's more to this world than what meets the eye. Like the death of your partner. Need I say more?"

"What do you want with me?" I push the omelet away without even touching it, but I'm not hungry. Not now.

"I want you to work for the Bureau of the Occult and the Other. Permanent assignment. It's already been cleared with your sergeant."

"I've been digging into Temple's case since I got out of the hospital, and I haven't gotten anywhere. What do you have?" Hope is a powerful motivator. She's also cruel and likes to flee as soon as you invite her in. But I grab on and don't let go.

I need the past three weeks to finally make some sense.

"Temple's case is...complicated. I can't let you touch it. But working for us, you'll finally be able to put your very unique *talents* to use. One-eleven Cargo Way. Be there in an hour."

———

Sin

"You cannot be serious." Hunger churns in my gut, and every moment I spend staring at Lieutenant Grayson Eve makes it harder to control myself. She slides a file across the desk, and I snatch it from her long fingers.

Zoe Dawes.

SFPD detective, junior grade, and currently riding a desk.

Thirty-four. Human.

The product of a Catholic grammar school, a Jesuit high school, and a private college.

Oh, she's going to love me.

Turning my attention back to Eve, I arch a brow. "You do realize pairing her with a *demon* isn't the best way to introduce her to the Bureau, right? Try one of the mages. Or a shifter."

"I'm not doing this for her, Sinclair. Your last assignment was a disaster. Hell, it was almost as bad as Tucson, and I won't save you from yet another raving mob after your head."

"That was a one-time lapse of judgement." Running a hand through my black hair, I wonder if I'll ever live that fiasco down. "If you had not insisted I work seventy-two hours straight, I would have fed on my own, and—"

Grayson rolls her eyes. "Enough with the excuses, Sinclair. I warned you there'd be consequences for your actions. Now, get the fuck out of here. Your new partner will be here at noon, and you might want to take care of your little...*problem* before then."

My *problem?* Fuck. Shoving the commander's door as hard as I can with my stomach twisting in on itself, I stalk through the bullpen.

Damn earthquake. Barely a three-point-five, but it was strong enough to cause everyone at Midnight Sin—the night-club I purchased a decade ago when I moved to San Francisco —to evacuate before I could settle on a snack for the evening.

I catch sight of my reflection in the two-way glass outside Interrogation Room Three and curse again. When I've fed, I'm normal enough. But as hungry as I am, I look like a cross between Matt Bomer, Jason Momoa, and Channing Tatum. That is if any of them had irises rimmed with crimson.

Bursting out of headquarters, I turn half a dozen heads—mostly women, but a few men as well—and three of them make a beeline straight for me.

"Are you a movie star?" The meek little mouse who reaches me first doesn't have enough power in her for a snack, let alone a full meal. But she might be able to take the edge off.

"No," I purr as I take her arm. "But I've often thought I should be. What role would you like me to play?" Steering her towards an alley, I scan the rest of the crowd, ensuring my glamour has taken hold and they see nothing as my tasty treat prattles on about how I'd make the perfect action hero.

"Or you could be a vampire," she says with a giggle. "And drink my blood. After you...bite me."

"What's your name, love?" I have one rule. I refuse to feed from anyone without knowing their name. Well, two rules. No killing. I'm a demon. Not a monster. Not anymore.

She gazes up at me with wide brown eyes. "L-Laura."

"It is a pleasure to meet you, Laura." Choosing the cleanest section of wall in the alley, I cage her, pressing my forearms to the bricks. "May I kiss you?"

"Y-yes," she stammers, and I crush my lips to hers.

Fuck. So sweet. And stronger than I'd thought. Her life force flows into me as our tongues dance together, and when my teeth scrape her lower lip, she moans. Or perhaps...that sound is coming from me.

Laura melts against the bricks, and soon, I have to wrap my arms around her slight frame to hold her upright. She claws at my shirt, desperate for more, but I probe her mind, seeing a husband, two children—adorable ones, even.

Enough.

Pulling away, I cup her cheek, my other arm still tight around her back. "Look at me, Laura."

She gasps as her gaze locks on mine. Unsurprising. With my feeding haze at its peak, my normally dark blue eyes are probably blood red. I let my lips curve and lower my voice. "Where were you going when you saw me?"

"The bank." Enraptured now, she gives me a lazy smile. "But we could go to a hotel?"

"No, sweetheart. Pay attention." After another brief kiss, I push into her mind once more. "You were headed to the bank, but then you heard a kitten crying from the alley. So you went to look for it. As soon as you reached this spot, the sound ceased. You waited a few moments but never found the poor little thing, so you returned to your errands. You will have no recollection of me, and will feel no guilt for what we...shared."

The memories firmly implanted in her mind, I break our connection and step back, using a small amount of my newly refreshed power to hide myself behind my glamour.

Laura shakes her head and blinks hard. "Here, kitty, kitty. Where are you, little one?"

After another few seconds, she shrugs, straightens her jacket, and almost floats back towards the bank. She'll remember nothing, other than how amazing she feels.

Letting my glamour slip away, I head in the opposite direction to find another very willing victim.

THREE

Fort Baker State Park.

Dead shifter off of Bunker Road.

CSI and Coroner en route.

Meet Agent Dawes there and DO NOT be your usual dickish self.

Commander Eve's terse message grates as I dab my lips with a handkerchief and watch my latest conquest toddle off, floating on the memory of shaking hands with one of the Helmsworth brothers.

Some days, my only joy comes from the little falsehoods I plant in the minds of those who keep me alive with their energy. Sated at last, I stride to my car, the lights on the Audi A3 flashing seconds before I sink into the buttery leather seat. Once I take the top down, I gun the engine and peel out into traffic.

After close to six hundred years exiled to the mortal realm, little excites me. The chase, the joy of feeding? Both provide temporary distractions, but most days, I am bored out of my mind. Bored enough to consider petitioning Gabriel to reduce my sentence. Though the celestial realm is the most droll place in all of creation. Now that my brother has left to make his place on earth—and mated himself to a warlock for fuck's sake —there's even less reason for me to want to return.

My work for the Bureau of the Occult and the Other is all that keeps me from stabbing my eyes out with a ball point pen. Other-on-Other crime can't be left to *humans*, but most of our cases are no more than run-of-the-mill. Werewolves, vampires, witches, and Fae can rob, steal, and maim as easily as humans. They are merely harder to catch.

Rolling to a stop at the light, I tap the in-dash controls. "Play case report: Fort Baker State Park."

A melodious voice oozes through the speakers. "As you wish, handsome. Victim is a twenty-five-year-old female tiger shifter. The body was discovered by two human runners approximately ninety-minutes ago. Mem-Clear has been dispatched, and the humans' statements have been recorded, along with their memory scans. A perception screen is in place along the perimeter, and all traffic has been diverted. CSI Team Two is en-route. Agent Zoe Dawes arrived on scene five minutes ago and is *not* awaiting further instructions."

Of course. I shift into a higher gear and take the curves at speeds only a being with preternatural abilities can handle. The tires leave the road as I careen around a bend, but I know my car—my sexy beast—and she can take more. Especially when I have so recently fed.

I cover the ten miles in under seven minutes, slam on the brakes, and squeal to a stop mere feet from the containment area.

The woman crouching by the body, elbows on her knees,

fingers steepled, with her auburn hair blowing in the breeze turns her gaze to mine.

A punch of power knocks me back against the seat, and her green eyes narrow and focus on me. There is something decidedly *other* about this human. Her stare draws me in and stirs something deep inside me. A long-ago feeling I cannot pinpoint or name. Or decide if I like.

Her photo did *not* do her justice. Rough-chopped red curls tumble around a thin, pale face. Freckles dot her nose, and bruised, puffy bags give her eyes a hollow look. The leather jacket hides her body and must be at least two sizes larger than she needs.

Rising, she unfolds her long, graceful legs, and I catch sight of a simple black blouse clinging to her breasts. Her full lips—unadorned—part, but the brief moment of desire that flashes in her eyes vanishes in a single breath.

She shakes her head. "Are you Sinclair?" she asks, jamming a palm on her hip.

"I am."

"You're late."

Zoe

Great. My partner's a pretty boy in a hot car with a swagger that could topple buildings. He strides over to me like he doesn't have a care in the world.

Someone's dead, dammit. Show a little fucking respect.

"You have a good reason for the delay?" I snap.

"A man has to feed." He bares his teeth, and I hold my breath, expecting fangs, but he merely smiles at me.

Working my jaw, I measure my words carefully. "Eat faster in the future. This one's hot."

"Care to explain?"

Unease slithers through me, and it takes all of my control not to rub the back of my neck. The gloves on my hands aren't exactly clean. Not after touching the corpse that had once been a beautiful young woman.

The handbook the commander gave me the previous morning kept me awake all night. A primer of sorts on *Others*. I read it cover to cover, fascinated, horrified, and excited all at the same time. And for the first night since I was released from the hospital, I didn't even think about touching the whiskey.

"A shifter's age is evident in her eyes. Faint circles radiate out from the pupils. The more lines, the older the shifter is."

"Gold star, *Agent*. Though most in my world learn such a thing by the time they are five." His smooth voice makes me want to melt at his feet and strangle him at the same time.

"Well, excuse me. Some of us were raised to believe *your* world was all in our imagination. My *point* is that you won't be able to tell me how old she is."

Sinclair arches a brow and crouches down. He pulls a glove from his pocket and snaps it over his long fingers before peeling back one of her eyelids. In that moment, his entire demeanor changes.

The flippant, irreverent playboy fades away, and he whispers something I can't hear before gently stroking his finger from her sculpted brow to her cheek.

Even after everything I've seen working for the SFPD, the shifter's empty sockets leave me off balance and queasy, and it appears Sinclair is affected too. "Hot enough for you?"

"Perhaps," he says as he rises and pulls off the glove. "But what I would truly like to know? What has your panties in such a twist, Agent? I do not think this is all because of the condition of the body."

"My *name* is Zoe. As for what's upsetting me? Your attitude, for one thing, *Sinclair*."

He stares at me, surprise in his midnight blue eyes. "Only the commander calls me Sinclair. You may call me Sin." His nostrils flare, which in a human, would indicate offense. But with whatever the hell he is? Who knows? "Eve rarely backs down, and she seemed quite insistent we work together. So, I am afraid we are stuck with one another."

At least he's honest.

"Looks like it." Turning back to the body, I stare at her. Beautiful—if not for the pallor of her skin and those damn missing eyes. Looking at her makes me feel like my entire existence is being drained away. Everything inside me gone. So I focus my attention on the surrounding area.

"Why would they dump her? Here? Did they want her to be found?" I walk the perimeter, feeling Sinclair—Sin—staring after me.

"They?" His nostrils flare again, and he shakes his head slowly. Okay. Now I *know* he's scenting something. "Is there some reason you believe this is the work of more than one? Or that the perpetrator—or perpetrators—wanted her to be found?"

"Look at this place." I wave my hand in a circle around me. "It's a well-used trail, the weather's almost perfect and has been for a week. There's zero chance the body stays hidden past 9:00 a.m. And there's not a damn bit of trace anywhere. That amount of care? Almost assuredly two people. Or more."

"She was not thrown from a vehicle," Sin muses and inclines his head. "The dirt is not disturbed. She is posed. Her feet are pointing due south. Palms up. Almost in supplication. There are faint bruises on her arms, but her body is clean—as if someone washed her." He pauses, then arches a brow. "Look at her, Agent—Zoe."

I do, and immediately, my stomach lurches. Sin takes a step closer. "Are you about to be ill?"

"This isn't my first rodeo," I snap. But his question isn't out of left field. It'll be a miracle if I hold it together for the next few minutes until we can get the fuck out of here.

"Then why do you appear as if you are about to lose your breakfast?"

The commander's last instructions echo in my head. *"Trust your partner, Agent Dawes. Sinclair is difficult, arrogant, and something you have never seen the likes of before. However, he is, above all...loyal."*

Pressing my hand to my stomach, to the scar from Temple's bullet, I swallow hard. "It's not the body. Not...exactly."

"What is that supposed to mean?" Sin tilts his head and narrows his eyes at me.

Fuck. His gaze packs a punch I'm not prepared for. The shifter...she was empty. Gone. A hollow shell. But Sin?

His eyes are full of heat. And pain. Regret. Longing. Curiosity. Resignation. So much more. Irises the color of a perfect sapphire, the outsides glowing a sky blue. And staring at him settles my stomach almost immediately.

Why?

"Zoe? Agent Dawes?" He holds out his hand, and my gaze pings between his strong fingers and his eyes. That's when I understand. Why the shifter affects me so deeply.

With Sin, everything I associate with a person, their soul, the very essence of their being is present. He's so much more complicated than the humans I'm used to dealing with, but he's definitely...here.

The shifter's body? It's missing all of that. Even after death, a person's soul remains for a time. I used to swear I could *see* it.

Until Temple warned me repeatedly not to admit that to anyone.

But with the shifter? She's not even a ghost. There's just... nothing there.

Frowning, I shake my head. "I'm fine."

After a beat, he nods. "Very well."

I can't help but ask. "What are you?"

"Something that should have never been born." Sadness laces his deep, lightly accented voice, but as I pin him with a hard stare, he sighs. "Incubus. Mostly."

"Do you have...talents?" He isn't telling me the whole truth, but though I've always been able to read people, to know whether they're lying, I have no idea what he's keeping from me.

"Talents?" His lips curve into a frown, and that strong, perfectly sculpted brow furrows, making me want to smooth the lines away.

"Incubus. You feed off of arousal, yes?"

He nods. "I can also feed off of fear, though I choose not to."

"What else? Can you read minds? Shit like that?"

Sin shoves his hands into his pockets. "I require arousal—and a name—to feed. I can, when connected to a person, see their memories in limited fashion. But only if they are willing or unawares—two states I can induce if necessary."

"How?" I need to know what I'm dealing with. What my *partner* can do. For me. With me. To me.

"Through vision and touch. I require both to compel someone—along with a pliant mind. I can give a person a 'nudge' if you will, to *want* to touch me. Something to tip them over the edge if they are wavering. And when I am hungry, I will automatically appear more...*appealing* to any humans around me. You have my word, however, that I never take from a human against their will."

"Is that because you can't or is it some moral code you live by?"

He's wary, but inclines his head. "My own moral code. Incubi are some of the world's most powerful demons. And the most dangerous. What is wrong, Zoe?"

I don't trust him enough to explain. Yet. Or to tell him just how green I am. "Nothing."

My curt response sets him off, and the low sound he makes could almost be described as a growl. "Fine. You know where the morgue is?"

"I'm assuming you're not referring to the San Francisco Medical Examiner's office."

Sin flashes me a wry smile. "Hardly. Follow me, then. I'm in the A3."

Like I hadn't noticed. But I keep my reaction to myself lest he leave me to find the morgue on my own. After all, he *is* a demon. I don't expect him to *ever* give me a straight answer.

How did I end up here? The only human working for an agency that calls itself BOO and following an incubus to a place no human knows about where I could disappear and never be heard from again.

Oh. That's right. I got shot by a man I should have been able to trust more than anyone else in the world. And then, I had the gall to investigate it.

FOUR

The CSI team—this one comprised of a mage and two warlocks —teleports the body directly to the morgue, so by the time we arrive, Dr. Breslin, the Bureau's coroner, is already partway through her examination.

My new partner looks a bit unsteady as she enters the room, but she swallows hard and schools her face into a mask.

"Initial findings?" I ask Breslin.

"Always hard to tell with shifters," she says. "Their injuries heal so quickly." Touching the dead woman's wrist with a metal probe, she nods as the device beeps in her hand. "Yep. Ligature marks."

"How can you tell?" Zoe asks, crouching so she can get a better look. "I don't see anything."

"This device reads the concentration of blood under the skin. Here," Breslin points to one slender wrist, "it registers a seven percent increase in broken blood vessels. Too low for the naked eye. I'd guess her ankles show the same marks. She was restrained a few days before she was killed."

"Cause of death?" I ask.

The doctor pulls back the shifter's lips, then runs a hand-held scanner over her torso. "Hmm. This looks like a puncture wound." She points to a small red dot on the side of the shifter's neck. "The tox screen will take at least four hours—and that's only if I'm lucky and get the sample in ahead of the vampire-orgy-gone-wrong in the Castro."

"Orgy?" Now that has the potential to be interesting. Unlike this case. Plus, the idea of seeing the very inexperienced Zoe Dawes wade through the aftermath of a vampire orgy makes my heart beat a little faster.

"That's Harv's case, Sin. And he's not sharing," Breslin says with a dry chuckle.

Shoving my hands into my pockets, I run through all the ways I could possibly convince the commander to transfer me as the doctor waves her assistant over.

The shifter is—was—beautiful. Long, dark brown hair, a lithe, toned body, and perfect skin. But a vampire orgy... The very idea leaves me salivating.

Breslin and her assistant slide the dead girl onto a sheet, then flip her. Zoe draws in a sharp breath, while I cannot seem to force my lungs to inflate at all. Her back is covered in fresh wounds. Long, thin welts with triangular-shaped markings at the ends. They healed enough to scab over, but only barely.

Breslin's assistant takes several pictures, and then the doctor brushes the shifter's dirty locks off her neck. "Well, this is interesting."

A fresh tattoo mars her skin. Fuck.

"*Mio maestro*," I whisper, and Zoe snaps her gaze to mine for a brief second until I shake my head.

No. I will *not* entertain the possibility. It cannot be him. But the small faery with luminescent wings and a chain wrapped around her neck is too much of a coincidence for it to be anyone else.

"What's that?" Zoe asks as she takes out her phone and snaps a photo.

Bloodlust, anger, and yes, fear, simmer under my skin, and both the doctor and my new partner jump at my snarl. "That... is a *brand*."

Fuck the vampire orgy. Harv can run with it. This case is mine—even if the Almighty herself offers me Heaven on a silver platter.

Zoe

Alone with the body after the medical examiner and her assistant head off to help with the victims of the vampire orgy—really? Vampires hold orgies?—my unease returns with a vengeance. The shifter is face up again, and her eyelids are peeled back, her empty sockets on display. Sin stares at her like he's seen a ghost.

"I should have known," he says under his breath. "I should have *felt* it. All these years. Centuries. Why now?"

"Um, hello? It's your partner? I'm still here." I take my small notebook and *thwack* it against his shoulder. Sin whirls on me, grabs it, and throws it across the room.

"*Never* do that again." His eyes are a deep crimson around the edges now, and the anger in their depths...it's terrifying. It also pisses me off. He doesn't get to intimidate me like that.

"Then don't shut me out, asshole. And tell me what you should have known." My stomach twists and roils, and if I have to look at the body another minute, I'm going to throw up.

Stalking across the room, I snatch my notebook off the floor and shove it back into my bag. Sin hasn't moved.

"You're really not going to tell me? Fine. I'll see you outside."

The Bureau's morgue is just like all the others I've been in. Nothing but stainless steel, frigid air conditioning, and weird smells that stick with you for hours—if not days. The green tiles remind me of my high school gymnasium, but the girls' locker room never had anything like the various tools lining the counters of this place.

It's all too much. The air in the hall is slightly fresher, but it's not enough to quell my nausea, and I replay the half an hour I spent at the crime scene. The poor couple who'd found the body had been sweet, and the techs had *wiped their memories*. Like something out of *Doctor Who* or *Men in Black*.

Who does that? Wipes memories?

Me, apparently. Or at least the organization I'm now a part of.

Bursting out into the brightness of late morning, I find a bench next to a planter of rose bushes. Something normal. Human. Even...pretty. I tip my head back and let the sunlight warm my cheeks, my eyes closed. Until a chilling image flashes behind my lids. A cage. In the dark. And I swear I can smell damp earth, moldy stone.

Get a hold of yourself, Zoe.

Forcing my eyes open, I scoot closer to the rose bushes and inhale deeply. I should *not* have read the BOO handbook while *Interview with a Vampire* played in the background. Big mistake.

A few moments later, Sin drops down onto the warm wood next to me. "That tattoo...the design is ancient. And I have seen it before."

"Where?" I tilt my head to find him staring up at the hills surrounding the city.

"Nowhere I can speak of. Trust me, Zoe."

His voice carries the weight of a long life—not that I have any idea how old he is—and when he says my name, a lump swells in my throat.

I don't know this man—this demon—but he's my partner, and I haven't been entirely straight with him either. If I want him to trust me, I have to trust him.

"It was her eyes."

"What?" he says.

"You asked me what was wrong earlier. At the crime scene." I glance up at him, only to find him staring across the street. A sliver of the bay's visible, and the blue-gray waters are calming. "I've seen bodies mutilated before. After weeks of decomp. You never forget that smell. It's awful, but it's part of the job."

"And her eyes still affected you that dramatically?"

"Yes." Running a hand through my curls, I search for some logic, some reason why, but come up with nothing. "It was like everything that made that shifter who she *was*...everything that made her a person...was gone. Like someone destroyed her from the inside out. And I've never seen a body that made me feel that way before."

Shock, anger, and understanding weave together, forming a deep rumble in Sin's chest, and I fall silent as I try to understand his reaction.

After what feels like an hour, he sighs. "There is more to this murder than meets the eye." At my cringe, he offers up a strained laugh. "Apologies. A most unintentional pun. Commander Eve should have warned us—warned me—about this before she sent us out there. Before she assigned you—"

"Hey."

Sin holds up his hand, "You *and* a demon whose past is forever linked to what we just saw in there." Rubbing the back of his neck, he ruffles his dark hair, and for the first time, I notice his fingers. They're burned in spots, the smooth, almost shiny skin at odds with the rest of him that appears to be perfection wrapped in a cocksure swagger. He shakes his head and turns his gaze to the parking lot once more.

His dark blue sports car stands out like a bird of paradise amid a flock of pigeons. Particularly next to my old coupe. I'm assuming from now on, *he's* going to want to drive.

After another few moments, he turns to me, his stare so deep, it's like he's searching my soul. Unlike inside, his irises are a glittering sky blue now, and I wish I felt comfortable asking him why they change colors. The section on incubi and succubi in the handbook was woefully short.

"I will not lie to you, Zoe. This case will be dangerous beyond all measure. Are you certain you can handle it?" he asks.

The question grates, but I can't blame him it. Not with how I acted at the crime scene. And in the morgue. *Rookies* puke at crime scenes. *Rookies* run out of the coroner's office and want to burn their nostrils with a blow torch.

"I've been in Homicide for eighteen months. Before that, I walked a beat. I was at the massacre down at the Pier back in January, and I've found my fair share of vagrants and junkies well after their expiration dates. I'm here now because..." I clench my hands hard enough for my short nails to dig painfully into my palms. "Because my partner tried to kill me, and I shot him." I don't look away, and though inside, I want to fall apart, I'll never let Sin see that happen.

With a curt nod, he says, "Very well. I hope neither of us regret this."

FIVE

Sitting next to Zoe, I try to make sense of her. Her file listed her as human, but the power behind her eyes? It is very real and very much...*other*.

Twice now, she has caused me to wonder if I have fed from her in the past. There is a familiarity to her mannerisms I cannot place, but yet, she is so unique, I know I would have remembered her.

As for why the body disturbed her so? There is more to that mystery as well. More than her discomfort with the shifter's missing eyes.

She leans forward with her elbows on her knees, staring at that little notebook in her hands. If I did not desire to keep her slightly afraid of me, I might do the same.

I'm drawn to her in a way I have only felt once before. Many centuries ago. I am always in control. I have to be. Now, more than ever. If the incubus bastard who called himself

Thorn was able to escape Hell, any distraction could be fatal—or worse.

Nothing prepares me for the assault of memories. Screams. Blood. Women. Men. Every manner of being in between. They all begged. Pleaded. Tried to bargain with Thorn to kill them and stop his endless torment.

I could not help them centuries ago, but if he—and the Fae woman he made his queen, Regina—are behind this dead shifter, I must end them. Now.

Fuck.

So much of that time is a blur. Regina's voice, so sweet and compelling as she used her Fae magic to wipe my mind of all independent thought. The unnatural, horrifying sensation of Thorn—*mio maestro*—using his power to compel me to carry out his sick desires. To terrorize and torture his victims, to bring them to auction where other, even more depraved demons would do...such horrible things to them.

During those two endless centuries, I was able to hold on to the thinnest shred of the man I'd once been. Not enough to resist him, but enough to drown in the endless, overwhelming guilt as I helped him destroy life after life and betrayed all I held dear.

Looking down at my hands, I can still see the blood. Somehow, I found a way to break free. But those memories are gone forever. My first clear recollection is dragging Thorn and Regina down to Hell and offering them to the Devil—along with my own soul as penance for my sins.

Surely, they could not have atoned. Hell isn't a place you simply *walk out of.* Beelzebub does not give out hall passes. The last demon who escaped—Stefan, I think his name was—well, he almost took the place down with him.

Movement in my periphery brings me back to the present, and I find Zoe running a hand through her hair, stopping at the back of her neck, and rubbing like she's trying to erase the memory of the shifter's tattoo.

My arm throbs, the place he marked me, and I force the pain away. With a hard, slow blink, I meet Zoe's gaze, and again, the power catches me unaware. Sucking in a breath, I put another inch of space between the two of us, though I ache to move closer. Something draws me to my new partner, something magical shimmering under her skin. In the depths of her green eyes. In her voice.

Does she know? About all that untapped power begging to be released?

With the grace that comes from complete and total control of my body, I rise and nod towards my car. "Follow me."

Zoe gets to her feet, but refuses to rush after me. Is she trying to assert some form of control? If she battles me, she will lose. Every time. Though...the fun we could have if she tried... One look and she could be a quivering mess at my feet. But I swore long ago I would never use my power on the unsuspecting again.

And Commander Eve would have my ass. Most days, that would be a small risk with a very large reward. But today? I will not step one toe out of line. This case is personal, and I will see if through. Even—or especially—if it ends my pitiful existence.

"Where are we going?" Zoe asks as she pulls her keys from her pocket.

The leather seat wraps me in comfort, and I drape my arm out the window and force a smile as she unlocks her own car. "Headquarters. I believe it is time for your first glimpse of the Bureau's red tape."

Zoe

Thank God for GPS. Sin's sleek, shiny car is a hell of a lot faster and more maneuverable than my old Civic, and he left me in the dust after less than two miles.

My meeting with Commander Eve took place in an enchanted building across town—in case I turned down her offer—so I've never been here before, and from the outside, BOO Headquarters looks like...well...nothing. A plain, concrete building with windows so heavily tinted, they're completely opaque.

By the time I park alongside Sin's A3, impatience hardens his already chiseled features.

"From now on," he says as he ambles towards the unmarked building, "I will drive."

My eye roll makes my head hurt. Sin holds the door for me, and once we're both inside, he frowns. "Is this your first time here?"

"Yes." I hold his stare, cataloging yet another variation in his eye color. At the moment, the outside of his irises are like the summer sky.

"Then prepare yourself."

As warnings go, it's pitiful, but when we round the corner and enter the bullpen, I realize there's nothing else he could have said. My jaw drops open, and Sin doesn't break stride. "I suggest you get yourself under control, Zoe. The leopards do not like to be *gawked* at.

If it were empty, this room would look like any other bullpen in the country. Beige walls, scuffed linoleum floors with a layer of grime no mop can remove, and the scent of stale coffee with an undercurrent of sweat. Even the desks look the same.

But the agents sitting at them? It's like a paranormal

menagerie. What can only be a vampire stares at me from two desks over, her lips curving into a smile and revealing sharp, glistening fangs. Her partner is...a ghost? She's wispy, almost translucent.

Sin's right about the leopards. A pair of them—twins if I had to guess—pin me with hard stares. They look like humans except for the spots and fur covering their bodies, their decidedly feline noses, and whiskers. I avert my gaze and follow Sin as he weaves through the bullpen and heads for a glass-walled office in the center of the large space.

Commander Grayson Eve paces, her lips moving rapidly, though I don't see anyone else in there with her.

When Sin bangs on the office door, she whirls around, taps her ear, and holds up her hand for him to wait. He ignores her and barges in anyway.

"I'm sorry, Governor," Eve says. "I'll have to call you back. My apologies." She yanks the earbud out and dumps it on her desk. "Sinclair, you'd better have a damn good excuse for bursting in like that."

He slams the door in my face, and as I'm about to lose my shit over my partner's rudeness, his shoulders heave, and he opens it again.

"Gee. Thanks," I say as I step inside.

"Zoe, this matter is between me and the commander," he says, ice in his tone. "But as my partner, you should know the danger this case will put you in. Now sit down and do not interrupt."

Commander Eve's expression is the only reason I don't go off on him. She's turned pale, her lips pressed together in a thin line and a muscle in her jaw ticking.

"Sinclair, if I ever hear you talk to your partner that way again, you will be suspended without pay for a month," she grits out. "I read Dr. Breslin's initial report. I know why you're here."

"How many others?" Sin demands. "She is not the first. Is she?"

Eve's shoulders slump, and she sinks down into an expensive chair with more levers and knobs than I've ever seen. "She is the second woman found dead this week. There was also a male, three weeks ago. Though as you know, it is almost assured that others are already missing."

"Three?" He paces, his hands balled into fists at his sides. "Tell me about all of them. Right fucking now."

Commander Eve pulls out a thick file and rests her hands on top of the plain, beige cover. "Before I tell you what's in here, I need to apologize to you, Zoe."

"Me? Why?" I sit up a little straighter. "I know I'm a complete rookie when it comes to the paranormal, Commander, but I assure you, I can handle—"

"That's not it." Her fingers curl slightly, and something shimmers over her skin. Are those...talons where her nails used to be? I stare, transfixed, until she clears her throat. "I have Eagle blood," she says simply as she flexes her hands and the talons fade into long, black fingernails.

"Oh. Uh, sorry."

"You will not last long here," Sinclair mutters under his breath, "if you do not learn to control your reactions."

"Well, maybe if you *prepared me* for what I was going to see..."

"Enough!" the commander slams her fist down on the desk and glares at both of us. "I can't tell if pairing the two of you was brilliance or idiocy. But it doesn't matter now. Sinclair, I realize you have only spent a few hours with your new partner, but have you told her anything about your past?"

He shakes his head, every muscle in his body strung so tight

I swear he's about to snap like a guitar string. "You know I do not like speaking of it. I have never told any partner."

"Well, that ends now." Eve presses a button at the corner of her desk, and the glass walls turn opaque, writing and images flaring to life all around the room. "Take a moment."

Rising, I follow the progression of dates and photos of so many missing all across the country—pictures from their lives. Happy, smiling faces. In some, the women have shifted—or partially shifted—into their animal forms, and in others, they look completely human. Except for the eyes, I realize. Every single one of them has an otherworldly quality to their eyes. The men, however...they all look human. Dates and cities are scrawled under each photo.

January - New York City. Twelve dead. Nine women, three men. March - Chicago. Twelve dead. Nine women, three men. May - New Orleans. Twelve dead. Nine women, three men. Dallas, St. Paul, Salt Lake City, Las Vegas, Phoenix, Los Angeles.

Nine cities. Over a hundred women and twenty-seven men.

"And now, you think whoever did all this," I wave my hand around the room, "is here in San Francisco? Why?"

"Because of the faery tattoo," Eve says. She picks up a tablet, taps the screen a few times, and the images and notes on the walls change. Now, the dead aren't so pretty. In many cases, they were only identified by DNA or dental records.

But in more than sixty percent of them, at least a partial tattoo was still visible on the body.

"Every ink sample is identical," she says. "And imbued with powerful magic. Not that we understand what it does.

"I don't know a lot about tattoos," I say, "but there can't be that many ink suppliers. I agree this seems like a high number, but are we sure—"

Sin clears his throat from the chair. He hasn't looked at any of the photos. In fact, he's staring straight ahead at the commander, and crimson rings his irises. "Shifters cannot be tattooed with regular ink, Zoe. The design will fade the moment they shift. It is their nature. That is very likely the purpose to the magic. Commander Eve was not talking about the chemical composition of the ink, but the magic infusing it."

"Oh." I look to Eve, and her blue eyes confirm Sin's words. "And our shifter?"

"The labs won't come back for another few hours," she says with a frown. "The magical analysis unit has never been one to rush. Not even for a case like this. But the design matches the others, as do the visual qualities—which alone are quite unusual."

"It must be him." Sin rises and walks over to the far corner of the room to a photo of a dead woman lying in a heap. She wears only a pair of lace panties, her neck broken and her head twisted at an unnatural angle. Jabbing the wall over her back, he snarls, "These marks, along with the ink...they prove it."

Joining him, I frown as I examine the broken lines of skin along the woman's back. "They're not standard whip marks, and today's victim had these same triangular-shaped injuries."

"That is because they are not from a 'standard' whip." His tone turns harsh and rough. "May I?" he asks as he holds out his hand for the commander's tablet.

She passes him the device, and he pulls up another photo. It looks a little like a thin, metal bar, but every two inches, there are other, odd protrusions almost shaped like triangles.

"What is that?" Sin rotates the image, and my stomach clenches. "Is that the letter T? In...cursive?"

"Yes. He calls himself Thorn. Part incubus, part something much, much stronger. He feeds off of fear, and he marks all of his victims so they can never forget they belong to him." Sin rubs his shoulder, then drops the tablet back on the commander's desk. "How long do we have?"

Eve frowns. "Unsure."

"Do not give me that bullshit!" Rounding the desk, Sin gets right in her face. "They *never* deviate from their pattern. Not in over a thousand years. The men are taken every four days. A week to *train* them. Then, nine women, one every third night! How. Many. Missing. Women?"

With each word, the edge to Sin's voice gets harder and harder, and I'm afraid he's about to grab the commander and shake her. I rush over to him and try to take his arm. "Stand down, Agent. Now!"

I don't think he hears me, but the commander lets out a screech that sends me to my knees with my hands over my ears.

Disoriented, I only catch a glimpse of pure white feathers, then the scent of blood, before Sin wraps his arm around my waist and helps me back to one of the guest chairs.

Blood wells along the edge of his jaw, and a handful of pinfeathers float through the air. Commander Eve's eyes are wild, but the rest of her? Shit. She's totally put together. Except for her long blond hair, which looks like she just touched one of those static balls at the county fair.

Gathering her tresses and securing them with a rubber band, she looks anywhere but at Sinclair. "Agent Dawes, I'm sorry you had to see that."

"You're...*sorry?*" My gaze pings between the two of them. Sin presses a handkerchief to the wound, his expression shuttered, yet the commander looks almost...exhilarated. "You just injured one of your own agents!"

"I lost control. And for that, I apologize to both of you," she says.

Shaking my head, I can't believe what I just witnessed. "Not good enough. Sure, he was being a complete dick, but—"

Sin growls, "I was justified in my actions."

"The hell you were," I say. "Is this how you deal with all of your problems? Combat? Because I don't want any fucking part of it."

I spin on my heel and make it halfway to the door before Eve's words stop me cold.

"We don't know the timeline because the first man to be taken broke the pattern. James Temple escaped, long enough to get to you, Agent Dawes. Long enough to beg you to kill him."

SIX

Zoe

"Temple..." I brace my hand on the door, Commander Eve's words echoing on a loop in my head.

Sin appears at my side. "Zoe? Agent Dawes? Sit down. You look...ill."

He offers me his hand, but I bat it away. I don't care how close I am to passing out or losing my breakfast, I won't do either of those things in front of a man who thinks it's cool to be called Sin.

He lowers his voice to a whisper, "If we are to work together, you will someday need to trust me."

I huff, but let him guide me back to the chair. My mouth is dry, and the headache doing a tap dance inside my skull shifts into double-time. I force my shoulders back and meet the commander's gaze. "Tell me what you know about Temple's...death."

"Very little," she says, her expression unreadable. "But his body bore the same mark as the other men taken over the past eighteen months." Tapping her tablet, she brings the image up on the wall behind her. Unlike the women's tattoo, which shows a female faery in chains, wings unfurled, head bowed, this tattoo is of a man carrying a whip. His wings are larger, and his face is hidden behind a black mask.

"Temple didn't have any tattoos," I say. When Sin arches a brow at me, I shake my head. "Get your mind out of the gutter. The man was afraid of needles. I had to go to the precinct's blood drive with him and recite old case notes just so he could donate a pint of O neg."

"This was on his forearm," Eve says, then flips to a photo of Temple's body in the morgue, naked from the waist up.

My stomach lurches, and I clench my fingers around the arms of the chair. *Don't lose it. Not now. You're a cop. Act like one.*

But seeing those same distinct whip marks across his chest —marks that couldn't have been made more than a day or two before he died—threatens to destroy my control. The photo flips to one of his back, and I swallow hard, tasting bile. "He...was tortured."

"Yes, Agent Dawes. As were all the other men across the country. Branded and whipped repeatedly," she says.

"To keep them in line." Sin's voice carries an edge of fury, and when I steal a quick glance at him, his irises are once more rimmed with red. "Thorn has a woman he works with. A Fae named Regina. His queen, of sorts. She wipes the victims' minds clean, then Thorn takes control of their thoughts, their bodies...until they go insane."

"Regina?" The unfamiliar name shocks me enough to stave off my impending vomit-fest, and I sit up a little straighter. "And how do you know about these people?"

"They are *not* people," he snarls, then softens his tone.

"Grayson, as much as I would prefer to never speak of this again, it is my story to tell. May we have the room?"

The commander looks as surprised as I am at Sin's conciliatory tone and the use of her first name. "Fine. I could use some flight time. You have an hour." She slides the tablet across her desk towards Sin. "Everything you need to know is in the case file. The Bureau's full resources are at your disposal, Sinclair. This reign of terror has to end. Here."

"It will," he says with a nod. "Or it will end me."

Sin

Telling Zoe about my past on the first day of our partnership? This is a mistake. But the dead man—James Temple—he was a San Francisco police detective, and apparently, Zoe's former partner.

Fuck. No wonder the photos affected her so.

She sits with her elbows on her knees again, staring at the autopsy pictures along the back wall.

"Thorn and Regina are two of the ancients."

"The ancients?" Zoe asks. Her face is still too pale, and the idea of glamouring her and making her forget all about the Bureau, about her partner's death, about me...? It is strong. But despite her lack of experience, she is curious and determined. And something about her calls to me. Demands to be respected. Honored, even. She lost someone she cared for. I must explain why.

"Demons."

She narrows her gaze at me. "Like you."

"*Not* like me." The words escape on a growl, and I punch

the wall hard enough to snap several bones in my hand. Zoe yelps as the pain zings up my arm.

"Shit. Sin. What did you—?" Her jaw drops open as I straighten my fingers and the bones start to knit back together in front of her. "That's..."

"When I have recently fed, I can heal many injuries in a few minutes," I say. "One of the benefits of being...what I am."

"You mean an incubus."

"No. I mean the other part of me we will not speak of." No one knows my true origins, and I certainly will not be sharing them with Zoe.

"You're seriously not going to tell me."

"No. It is not relevant to this case. Suffice it to say, Thorn and Regina are the two most vile demons ever to walk the earth. He was 'born,' if you will, at the beginning and is older than any of us. She...well, he caught her in his thrall soon after."

"The beginning of what?" Zoe pulls her notebook out of her pocket, but I shake my head, and she drops it on the commander's desk with a huff.

"Of everything. The universe, the whole of creation, is based on balance. Good and evil. Black and white. Yin and yang. For every good thing the Almighty created, something evil sprang into existence as well."

The weight of the past, of my sins, exhausts me, and I sink down next to Zoe, staring at the commander's glass paper-weight. It is shaped like the moon, and stirs memories of begging for my death while the demon who insisted I call him *mio maestro*—my master in Italian—branded me.

"So, they're really old. And what? Really strong? Like vampires?" Zoe asks, the curiosity in her voice helping me to focus.

"Thorn is part incubus. Fuck. For all I know he may be a full-blood incubus, but unlike most incubi and succubi who feed off of arousal, he feeds only on fear." I run a hand through my hair, suddenly greatly appreciative of the ability to control my own body and mind. "Alone, he is more powerful than any demon I have ever known. But with Regina at his side, they are unstoppable."

"No one's unstoppable."

I spin her chair to face me and let my anger rise to the surface. "Listen to me, Zoe. They are. Regina can compel any human or *other* with only her voice. Force them to do almost anything she wishes. They are helpless to resist. Thorn? He is even worse. I told you I could influence my...chosen targets with my talents? See some of their thoughts?"

She nods, her lower lip trapped between her teeth.

"Thorn can see *everything*. He can force a man or woman to stab themselves in the heart with as little effort as you would spend to bat away a fly. And he lives to *terrorize* his victims until they go mad from fear. Every. Single. Moment. Pure torture. These two are nothing you have ever seen. And you will *not* go up against them. Ever. You will lose, and then you will die."

"Don't tell me what to do, Sin." She shoves back at me, springs to her feet, and stomps over to the wall behind the commander's desk. "This was my partner. The man who trained me." Jabbing at Temple's photo, she chokes back an oath. "And I had to kill him. I deserve to know why."

"Because once you are under Thorn's thrall, you are nothing. No one. Whoever you were before? That is gone. Wiped away so thoroughly, your soul rebels and drives you insane. It is the worst kind of pain, knowing you used to be someone else—someone better—but having no memory of that time and no hope of ever reclaiming it." My chest heaves, my throat tight. "The moment Regina first spoke to your partner—for she always initiates the contact—his death was assured. You...you showed him mercy."

Zoe doesn't move, her expression unreadable, but when I take a wheezing breath, I can taste her emotions. It would be so easy to glamour her, and between healing my broken bones and reliving the worst experiences of my very long existence, the temptation is strong. Turning away, I struggle for control—something I have not had to do in centuries.

"Sin."

She's close enough to drop her voice to a whisper. "How do you know all of this?"

My fingers shake as I shed my jacket and unbutton the cuff of my dress shirt, rolling it up to my elbow. Facing her once more, I hold out my arm. "It took me years. To scar the skin this deeply. But the ink is spelled. It returns. Every decade or so, it seeps through. When that happens, I take two weeks somewhere full of people. Somewhere wild. Las Vegas. Monte Carlo. Ibiza. Somewhere I can find a soundproofed room to hide my screams as I burn my flesh over and over again. Somewhere...I can feed to my heart's content to replenish my strength each night until I no longer have to see the reminder of the *thing* he made me into."

Zoe's green eyes take on a slight shimmer as she lays her hand over the scars. The familiarity of the touch, the empathy in her voice, do something to my heart I am ill prepared to handle. Emotions I have not felt since I descended into Hell flare to life, and I look away. Until her fingers tighten subtly. "You? Were...?"

"Yes. For hundreds of years, I was his slave. And the things I did..." I clear my throat when my voice cracks. "I have only scraps of memories. A blessing I am certain I do not deserve. After I fought my way free from his control, I dragged him to Hell. Both of them. But one does not simply drop two of the most powerful and vile creatures in existence at Beelzebub's doorstep and walk away. Hell's Prince is too cunning. Too desperate for more souls to torture for all eternity."

Her breath hitches, and she locks her gaze with mine. "You were trapped there with them."

SEVEN

Zoe

My partner has been to Hell. And not in the figurative sense. My fingers still rest over the heavily scarred skin on his arm, and I pull away, my cheeks flushing hot. "I'm...um...sorry..."

Sin waves his hand away like finding out you're working with someone from the Underworld is an everyday occurrence. Maybe it is for *him*, but not for me. "You could not have known. What remains to be seen is whether Commander Eve knew before she sent us out on this call."

He picks up the tablet and taps the screen a few times, then gives me a curt nod. "All of the files have now been transferred to my secure online vault. I would rather not encroach on the commander's private space any longer. There are soundproof conference rooms upstairs. We should claim one for the next few hours."

Logic. I can work with logic. And detachment. His eyes are mostly one color again—a sapphire blue, but there's still a hint of red surrounding them. His voice is cool and professional, and he straightens his shoulders as he buttons his sleeve, then shrugs into his jacket.

His defined muscles stretch the crisp black shirt. I shouldn't look, shouldn't notice, but even as shocked as I am by his admission, I'm not dead. And it's been a long damn time.

Stop it, Zoe. He's your partner. And a demon. Let's not forget that part.

He pulls a keycard from his pocket. As he passes it to me, our fingers brush, and all of a sudden, it's like someone lit candles all around the room. Light flickers over the back of his hand, and I think I hear him whisper, "Please, love. Hold on."

"What did you say?" Jerking back, I stare up at him. "Hold on?"

"I said nothing." Sin narrows his eyes, then nods at the rectangular piece of plastic. "That keycard works on all of the electronic locks in this building. You will need it. Even for the bathroom."

Spinning on his heel, he heads for the bullpen, and I follow as he weaves among pairs of desks arranged in neatly defined rows. "That is yours," he says, gesturing as he pulls out my chair.

The desk across from me is bare save for a keyboard, mouse, and monitor. Nothing personal. No pictures, plants, or even a coffee cup. Mine is just as empty, but I have a photo of my grandmother and my favorite pen in my bag. It's something at least.

"Aren't we—"

"We are. I thought you might want to see your workspace." Sin lifts his shoulder. "If not, follow me."

"I don't know about you, but I need coffee." I veer off when the scent of stale brew grows stronger and head into the small break room area where I promptly run right into a seven-foot-tall man with *fur* sticking out of the cuffs of his dress shirt. Oh my God. He's...a yeti.

"You the new recruit?" he asks. His voice is deep and scratchy, making his words sound almost like he's growling. "Kunchin."

I stare at his palm—his very large, very leathery palm—for a second longer than I should, then snap myself back to the present. "Zoe Dawes."

"Human, huh?" Kunchin chuckles at my shock. "Eve sent out a memo. You're the first one we've had."

Nodding, I glance at the coffee machine. "I don't suppose it's any good?"

With a snort, Kunchin sidesteps me and opens the fridge, retrieving a carton of vanilla creamer. "If it were anything but swill, you wouldn't catch me using this sugary shit. Want some?"

Behind me, Sin clears his throat. "Zoe? This case is not going to solve itself."

"I'm not going to solve it either if I don't get some caffeine in me," I snap back. "And yes, Kunchin. I'll take some of that 'sugary shit.'"

FRUSTRATION STIFFENS Sin's shoulders as we climb the stairs to the second floor. Eight rooms line a long hallway, a few with red lights glowing next to small screens on the wall. We find an empty space, and he swipes another keycard over the lock and pushes the door open, letting me enter first.

It's like some futuristic *Star Trek* bridge in here. Along the far wall, a bank of computer terminals stretch out, and the whole room has a bluish hue from the BOO screensaver. Shockingly, the Bureau's logo isn't a ghost, but a pair of swords crossed over a rather normal-looking badge. Speaking of badges...

"Do we have...credentials?" I ask. "If we're interviewing a witness, we need some proof of who we are, right?"

Sin pulls a small leather folio from his pocket and flips it open. The Bureau's badge shines in the blue lights. He's not smiling in the photo. Quite the opposite. Which, I guess is his default look, so it's fitting.

"Was anyone going to bother to set me up with one of those?" Rolling my eyes, I sink down into one of the chairs—fully ergonomic and so comfortable, I think I could fall asleep in it—and pull out my notepad.

"The commander has done a smashing job preparing you for your first day," he says with a scowl. "I assume you have not signed any of the release forms either?" When I shake my head, he sighs. "After we finish here, I will take you down to Other Resources. Eve is not usually this...sloppy."

Sin presses his index finger to a sensor in the middle of the table, and a computerized female voice fills the room. "Welcome, Agent Sinclair. Please say a command."

"Display Fort Baker case file, autopsy notes, and photos on Screen One."

Within five seconds, an entire wall is filled with images of the crime scene, the tattoo, and the shifter's hollow eye sockets. My stomach pitches, and I look away.

"Can we hide the picture without her eyes?" I ask, hating the weakness in my tone. "At least until we need it?"

Surprise laces his response. "Computer, close Image 56-B." After a few seconds, he says, "The photo is gone. This is visceral for you, is it not?"

"If you mean illogical and annoying and something I can't control? Yes." Cupping my hands around the steaming mug of over-brewed, bitter coffee, I use the familiar scent to ground me.

He frowns. "What are you?"

I almost drop the mug as I jerk my head up. "Human."

"Are you certain?" Sin leans closer, and though two feet of table separate us, I can *feel* his presence. Like its always been there. Right next to me. Or...close by anyway.

"Yes! My parents were human, my grandmother was human." He doesn't appear convinced. "Don't you think I'd *know* if I weren't? Shit. From the amount of information Commander Eve had on me before she recruited me, *she'd* know. Pretty sure those files went all the way back to the time I threw up all over my teacher in kindergarten."

Sin inclines his head. "Likely. The Bureau does not take chances. Not after the massacre two hundred years ago."

"Massacre?" He's hazing me. Trying to get a rise out of the newbie. He has to be.

"Computer, display images from the Registration Riots on Screen Two," he says, and oh my God. Calling it a blood bath is an understatement.

"Wh-what happened?" I push to my feet, equal parts horrified and curious. The bodies are torn apart, so little remaining that most aren't even identifiable as people any longer. "Are those...claw marks?"

"That is the result of the human government's attempt to control the Other. For a brief time, all members of the Bureau were required to *register* with the World Oversight Council. Not long after the law passed, several Council members with prejudices against our world decided we were not fit to remain free."

"Were you there?" If he had any part in this... I don't know how to feel about the images I see on the screen. But I need to know if my partner's capable of this level of violence.

"No. Most of the deaths came at the hands of two bear shifters with anger management issues. Hence our very extensive screening process. The humans may have been in violation of every Other rights law in existence, but they did not deserve...*that*." His sigh is only inches from my ear, and I spin around in shock as he adds, "The vampires wanted to glamour them all. But that is not our way. Nor should it be."

We're so close, I can smell his soap. Or cologne. Or maybe that's just him. Whatever it is, it's intoxicating. Like leather and fine scotch, along with a hint of smoke, and I breathe deeply. He lifts his hand, as if he's about to touch my cheek, but then blinks hard and takes a step back.

"You weren't about to try to *glamour* me, were you?" I ask.

With his fingers splayed over his heart, he focuses his stare on me, and the ring of red around his irises deepens. "I swear to you, Zoe, I will not feed from you without your permission, and I will *never* influence you. Your mind is your own and always will be."

"And I'm supposed to believe you?" His tone and his body language tell me he's being truthful—or they would if he were human. I'm just so out of my element with a demon as a partner I don't know if I can trust my own senses.

"Believe what you want." Sin drops his hand and returns to his seat at the table. "It is time for us to get to work."

EIGHT

Two hours later, Zoe is on her third cup of coffee and she has filled two entire screens of the conference room wall with notes.

"So, across nine cities, the timeline stays almost exactly the same?" Zoe shakes her head. "Three men, then nine women. Four days between the abductions of the men, three between the women. But there's no pattern to when the bodies are discovered. Why not?"

I rub the growing ache in my forearm, screams overwhelming my memories. A pretty young wolf begging me to kill her. I can still see the rune Thorn carved into her forehead to stop her from shifting. I had my hands around her throat, ready to end her suffering when Thorn found me and compelled me to release her.

I still bear scars from that day. One of the few memories from my time as his prisoner that has always been clear in my mind.

"Sin?"

Another voice, another time. So faint I can barely hear it. *"Sin. Help me. I can fight him. I know I can."*

"Hey. Partner. Sinclair. Did you hear me?" Zoe asks.

I dig my fingers into the burned remains of my tattoo, using the pain to keep me focused. "Some of them resist longer than others. I cannot say for certain, but from the bits and pieces I remember, the women are not taken until all of the men are mindless slaves. Those of the *Other* are strong, Zoe. Stronger than humans, and Thorn takes no chances. He insists the men be the ones to secure the women. To beat them. To arrange for their transport." A violent shudder causes my chair to scrape along the floor, and I push up and start to pace.

"Transport? To...where?" Zoe asks.

I pause and take a deep breath. I do not want to tell her the rest, but from the look on her face, she is starting to put the pieces together on her own. "Somewhere other demons, sometimes even humans, pay for the opportunity to do...whatever they please to these women."

Her shoulders hunch inward, and she shivers. "Wh-whatever they please. Like he sells them for sex?"

How I wish it were only that. "Often. Sex is profitable. That has not changed throughout all of history. Every culture and every creature has a dark side. Most never give in to their basest desires, but there are enough who do. Thorn feeds off of terror, misery, and pain. He delves into his victims' minds, into the deepest, darkest recesses where we hide all of our fears. And he uses them, *consumes* them. Until the women—and the men—can no longer muster the will to live."

Across the table, Zoe shrinks further inward and covers her mouth with her hand. A choked sound might be a sob, but she swallows hard and straightens, though when she speaks, her voice is not steady. "So that's why he doesn't just stay in one place and keep the women...for as long as they're marketable." She grimaces. "That's a horrible way of putting it, but, most sex trafficking rings are in it for the long haul. Until the women—or girls, really—age out or are so damaged no one wants them, they're sold over and over again."

"The mind is beautiful, complex, and resilient," I say, staring at a photo of another dead shifter, this one from Washington D.C. "To a point. What do you fear most, Zoe? You do not need to tell me, but do you know?"

Her answer is only a whisper, so faint I must strain to hear her. "Losing who I am. Like...Temple did."

I stop pacing. The urge to comfort her, to touch her, is so strong, I almost reach out and lay a hand on her shoulder. "The women are killed—either by Thorn or by their own hands—when they have lost so much of themselves, they go insane."

Zoe's emotions infuse the room. Compassion. Understanding. The scent...it is both familiar and strange, comforting and disconcerting. She tips her face up to meet my gaze. "Sin, did you...?"

"Yes. I tried. More than once. And I failed at every turn."

I need air. To move of my own free will. To feel the wind, the sun on my face. To be surrounded by nothing but silence rather than the horrors in my head. And to figure out how the fuck Thorn escaped from Hell. Before Zoe can stop me, I am out the door, taking off at a run for the stairs.

I can move faster than most humans, and I draw on a bit of my glamour to hide me from my partner's sight as I speed through the bullpen.

By the time she slips through the Bureau's doors, the Audi's purring like a kitten, and I slam my foot down on the gas pedal and speed away as Zoe calls my name.

FROM HIGH ON the hill overlooking the Golden Gate, the San Francisco Bay appears as if it is full of glittering diamonds. A stiff breeze stings my cheeks, reminding me I am alive and free.

I should not have run out on Zoe, but if I had stayed in that stale, windowless room for another minute, the darkness inside me would have taken over.

Pulling out my phone, I call my brother. In London, it is close to midnight, but I need information, and Maddox is the only one who might be able to get it for me.

"Sin?" His deep voice is rough, yet it soothes the cracks in my armor and allows me to take an easier breath. "What's wrong?"

"He has returned."

"Who?"

In the background, Mad's lover, Killian, tells him to come to bed, but Mad hushes him. When the distinctive sound of kissing carries over the line, I roll my eyes. "Maddox."

"Hang on, brother. It's late. We were..."

"I do not need to know what you were doing," I snap, then regret my ire. "My apologies. It has been a trying day, and I need information from Gabriel."

A door shuts wherever Maddox is, and he clears his throat. "I haven't spoken to Gabriel since I chose Killian over returning to the celestial realm."

"Mad, the demon...the one who... Fuck. Thorn is back."

"Killian!" Maddox shouts for his witch and switches the call to video. The two of them huddle close together in front of the camera. "There's a demon after Sin."

Killian frowns, then runs a hand through his mussed hair. "I thought Sin was part demon."

"I am half-incubus, witch. And I do not know if Thorn is

after *me*. But he *is* after men and women of the Other and has been for eighteen months now."

"Shit," Mad says. "Are you sure?"

"Yes, I am sure! Do you think I would make something like this up?" I want to throw the phone off the cliff, but that would solve nothing.

Maddox sighs and shakes his head. "Of course not. Does he know you survived?"

"Your guess is as good as mine. He is aware I brought him and Regina to the Underworld. That I struck a bargain that trapped me in Hell right along with them. But we were not tortured together. For the past eighteen months, he has been moving from city to city across the United States, and now, he is in San Francisco. Two bodies have already been found. If I do not stop him, he will continue his reign of terror across the world. I did not spend centuries in Hell to damn thousands more to my fate. I *need* to speak to Gabriel."

A hand claps me on the shoulder, and I whirl around.

"Well, if that is all you wanted, you could have simply asked."

The archangel stands before me, his long white robes and flowing hair billowing in the breeze. I stagger back a few steps, his presence almost painful, and meet Mad's gaze on the screen. "I have to go." Ending the call, I swallow hard. "Hello, Gabriel."

NINE

Sin

"You called?" Gabriel says with an air of superiority to his tone I have not missed in my centuries of banishment. "I do not enjoy this realm, Sinclair. Get on with it."

I grab the archangel by his robes and shove him against my car. "The incubus piece of shit calling himself Thorn. Why is he no longer in Hell?"

With a roar, Gabriel knocks me back ten feet, and I land on my ass in the dirt at the edge of the cliff. Fuck. Any closer and I would have gone over. "You forget your place, half-breed."

"And you forget that the Almighty welcomed my father into the celestial realm. If you are going to insult me, do so for my choices, *not* my parentage." I brush off my black pants as I give Gabriel a wide berth lest he decide to teach me yet another lesson. "I went to Hell for almost two centuries so that abomination would never be free again. Yet he has returned to the mortal realm and has been terrorizing and murdering for over a year now. Care to explain?"

Even with his wings hidden, Gabriel carries himself like the Almighty's chosen one. Shoulders straight, chest puffed out, and somehow staring down his nose at me, even though I am a full two inches taller. But as he processes my words, his countenance shifts and his brow furrows. "I was not aware. Are you certain it is the demon? Humans are quite often horrible creatures, Sinclair. One or more of them could simply be abducting those of the *other* for sport."

Pulling out my phone, I bring up the photo of the dead police officer's arm with Thorn's signature tattoo. "If this is not his work, someone is doing a bang-up job of impersonating him. No human alive should be aware of this mark or its symbolism."

With a sharp breath—breath he technically does not need to take—Gabriel narrows his eyes at the image. Anger makes his alabaster skin glow, and the rumble in his chest is not a sound I have ever heard him make before. Not even when he banished me to this realm until I had *atoned* for my misdeeds.

"This should not be possible," he says, almost to himself. When he returns his gaze to mine, disdain and disgust twist his normally perfect features. "I will have to pay Lucifer a visit. I *hate* the trip to the Underworld. If this is all some human playing at demonology, I will be very pissed off."

Before I can reply, he vanishes, leaving only a stirring of dust in his wake.

***

I HAVE BEEN GONE TOO LONG, and the litany of text messages does nothing to assuage my guilt. Six from Maddox and four from Zoe. Maddox will forgive me. Zoe? That is doubtful.

Tracked down your phone number, finally. Don't suppose you're coming back anytime today?

Leaving all the research to someone who's never used the Bureau's computer system before is bullshit, Sin.

Found Other Resources. No thanks to you.

Her final message sends a storm of guilt washing over me.

The last time a partner went dark on me, he died. If you're not dead, you better have a damn good explanation.

On my way back to headquarters, I ring Maddox.

"Sin? What the bloody fuck?"

"Do not lecture me, Mad. I certainly did not expect Gabriel to *hear* me." Taking a corner on two wheels, I floor it up one of San Francisco's more challenging hills. "He knows nothing. Yet. But he is on his way to see Lucifer as we speak. Or so he says."

"He's an archangel," Mad replies, as if I've forgotten. "He does not lie."

"I would not be certain of that. Gabriel can twist the truth to his liking with ease."

"When will you know? I'm worried about you." As I stop at a red light, I laugh off his concern, but he's having none of it, and his frustration carries over the transatlantic connection. "Fine. Do things all on your own. Like you have always done. It's not like we're family or anything."

The car's display flashes *Call Disconnected,* and I stare at it for so long, someone behind me honks. When did the light turn green?

Maddox hung up on me.

I cannot pry that thought from my head until I pull into the Bureau's parking lot and search for Zoe's old coupe. Fuck. She is not here. I do not know why I am surprised. It is well after 5:00 p.m.

"I will apologize to her in the morning," I say to no one. Tonight, I have some investigating of my own to do.

Zoe

My apartment feels smaller than usual. Probably because as little as a few hours ago, I thought I could find a place at the Bureau. Somewhere I'd belong. Until Sin ran out on me and didn't respond to any of my messages.

Kunchin showed me down to Other Resources, also known as the Bureau's Personnel Department. The Yeti's a cool guy. Maybe tomorrow I'll get up the courage to ask him how he blends in with the rest of the human world when he investigates Otherworldly crime. Because I *know* I'd remember seeing him walking around the city.

Oh shit. Have I been Mem-Cleared?

The couple at the park this morning weren't allowed to leave until they'd spent time with the crime scene techs. Before Sin arrived, one of them—a mage—had explained that they take brain scans of any human witnesses, then wipe their memories of all existence of the *other*. I couldn't watch them do it, and now I wish I had.

After I lock the door and strip out of my jacket, I head for the kitchen, wondering if I'll ever forget the things I saw today. So many photos. Most of them showing women brutalized so badly, they were unrecognizable. Some were only identifiable by dental records or a lingering bit of magic near their final resting places.

The half-empty bottle of whiskey beckons me, but now that I know what this Thorn asshole is capable of, I need to be clear-headed, so I start a fresh pot of coffee instead.

Kunchin didn't just show me Other Resources. He taught me the Bureau's computer system. Even got me set up with my own secure cloud storage drive. So after I change into a pair of sleep shorts and my favorite SFPD t-shirt, I pour myself a large mug of my favorite brew—a Peruvian single-origin—and curl up in bed with my laptop.

From what I've gathered, both from talking to Kunchin and scanning the news articles in the weekly shifter newspaper—the existence of which nearly had me falling out of my chair earlier today—the shifter community in San Francisco keeps to themselves. And they hate the handful of shifters who work for the Bureau. Some dust up with a tiger shifter agent who hassled one of the leopards working the sex trade in the Tenderloin.

"You'll have more success without a shifter on your investigative team," Commander Eve says when I petition her for a new partner who's at least fifty percent less asshole and a hundred percent more shifter. "This is a delicate case, Agent Dawes. Sinclair knows that. But from what he has told me of his history—which is not much, by the way—it is also deeply personal for him. He will come around." The corner of her mouth curves slightly. "He is, despite all evidence to the contrary, a good man. Plus, he knows better than to cross me."

I hope she's right.

As I search for the case notes from New York, a hint of nausea crawls up the back of my throat.

Calm down, Zoe. You haven't even opened the file yet. Get it together.

But suddenly, I feel trapped. My muscles lock, my breath catches in my chest, and I can't even blink. Panic takes over, and every cell in my body screams with a pain more intense than anything I've ever felt before.

Struggling against my own mind, I fight my way free of the blankets and hit the floor, my fingers digging into the well-worn carpet. The rough sensation helps me focus, and my heart rate slows, my thoughts clear, and I'm left with a hollow ache deep inside my soul that I fear will never fade away.

TEN

Sin

Loup Noir is one of the more reputable shifter hangouts in the city. Catering to a high-end crowd, the bar sells twenty-dollar drinks and appetizers on tiny plates that would barely feed a child, let alone any of the patrons who burn calories at twice a human's rate.

Steps from the bar, two female panthers, who look entirely human save for their sleek black fur and golden eyes, stop me. "You don't belong here, demon," one of them purrs as the other bares her sharp teeth.

I hold up my hands, then slowly reach into my coat pocket. "Bureau business." They tense until I flip open my badge, then one raises a delicate hand and smoothes down the raised fur on the top of her head.

"Go tell Jinx there's a Bureau agent here," she says, and the other panther pads off, a red bodysuit hugging her curves. "I'm Dion. I'd say it was a pleasure, but lying leaves a bad taste in my mouth. What do you want?"

Pulling out my phone, I bring up one of the less jarring photos of the dead shifter. "Know her?"

Dion's eyes widen, taking on a shimmer, and she lets out a low, mournful yowl largely hidden by the loud dance beat surrounding us. With a nod towards the end of the bar, she turns on her stiletto heel and strides away.

This corner of the club is slightly quieter, and she flashes two fingers to the bartender. He pours her a double shot of vodka, then fixes his perfectly round eyes on me. I can't tell what he is, but I'd guess some form of lizard. Or perhaps a chameleon. "What'll it be?"

"Zacapa 23. With only *one* cube of ice."

Dion tosses back her drink in a single swallow. The bartender refills her glass before snagging the bottle of rum from a high shelf. "Thirty bucks," he says, holding out his hand.

A fucking rip-off, even if this is some of the best rum in the world. "Keep the tab open." Drink in hand, I return my focus to Dion. "Who is she?"

"Jacinda. She was a regular on cats-only nights." Dion sniffs, a single tear glistening on her lashes. "A wolf accosted her years ago—beat her up after she refused to sleep with him— and she only trusted those of the feline persuasion."

The last word rumbles deep in her throat, and if I were not on the job, I would give serious thought to pursuing her—at least for the night. Instead, I swirl the rum in the snifter, letting the familiar butterscotch scent center me.

"When did you last see her?"

Dion leans halfway over the bar. "Bastian? When was our last cats-only night? Ten days ago?"

The bartender shakes his head. "Eleven."

"Anyone who might have seen her *after* that night? Did she have friends? Family in town?" Downing the rest of the rum, I nod at Bastian for another.

"I don't know. I'll have to ask Jinx. She's the owner here, and she knew Jacinda better than I did." Dion's voice isn't as smooth now, and she knocks back the second vodka, then slams the glass down on the bar top. "Jacinda was so sweet. Timid. What...what happened to her?"

"The Bureau is still investigating. Where do I find Jinx? She and I need to have a talk."

JINX IS A TALL, willowy redhead wearing a black chainmail dress that dips low between her breasts before falling all the way to the floor. She rounds her desk in the club's back office and offers me her hand. "You are Sinclair?" she asks, her amber eyes trained on me.

"Agent Sin."

Her grip is strong, and as she leans closer, she sniffs once. "Incubus? And...something else. These walls are warded, Agent Sin. Glamour is not possible inside this room, so I suggest you do not try."

"My *talents* are for personal use only. If I relied on them to do my job, I would be a piss-poor investigator." I bristle at the suggestion I would influence a potential witness, but I suppose it is not an unreasonable assumption. "You knew a tiger shifter named Jacinda?"

Jinx's eyes darken, and she presses her red lips together for a moment before she takes a seat and motions for me to do the same. "You said 'knew.' Jacinda's dead?"

"Her body was found this morning at Fort Baker park. One of your floor managers, Dion, said Jacinda was here eleven days ago. I need to know if you saw her after that night."

"I didn't. I had a family emergency and left the Feline Fest a little after nine. Jacinda was sitting at the bar with Dion. I called her this past weekend but she didn't answer, and I left her a message. I worried, but she traveled often for work. Pharmaceutical sales. I assumed..." Jinx shakes her head. "I should have checked on her. What happened?"

"I cannot share details of an ongoing investigation. Do you have her address? Phone number? Names of her other friends?"

"Y-yes. I can give you all of her contact information." Jinx scribbles on a Post-it note, then grabs a second one and adds her own phone number. "Call me any time, Agent Sin. Jacinda and I weren't terribly close. She only moved to San Francisco a few months ago. But she was a kind and sweet soul, and I wanted to get to know her better."

"I will." Rising, I tuck the papers into my pocket. A vague sense of guilt over questioning Jinx and Dion without my partner lingers in my gut, but I lack the patience to explain the nuances of the shifter world to her tonight. I can sense the grief flowing from the jaguar still sitting at her desk, and before I slip through the door, I add, "I will find her killer and they will pay."

WITH NO WORD FROM GABRIEL, the prospect of going back to my penthouse apartment leaves me unsettled, so I take a seat at the bar and order another drink. Three hours later, midnight approaches, and sobriety is a distant, fuzzy memory.

Other than the bartender, not a single shifter has spoken to me, but that affords me the opportunity to observe. The wolves and hyenas do not mix with the cats, but the bears and dragons don't care. They'll dance, flirt, and make out with anyone.

"Another," I slur to Bastian, but he shakes his head.

"Sorry, man. You're cut off. Did you drive here?"

The chameleon blinks so quickly, I struggle to focus and

snarl as I dig my keys out of my pocket and hold them over my head. "I am d-drunk. Nnnot ssstuuupid. I will walk. Bill. Now."

Anger helps sharpen my words, and I scribble my name on the check, tuck my card and keys back into my pocket, and stumble towards the door.

Halfway there, a sweet, melodious voice floats just under the music.

"You want to come with me now, dearie. I will take care of you."

I know that voice. And the solicitous tone with an undercurrent of pure evil. I thought she had stolen all my memories of her, but apparently, some were merely buried. Regina. I scan the club, desperate to discern if this is all in my head or if she is truly here.

"Did you drive here, my sweet girl? Where did you park? Tell me now, and forget about your friends."

Fuck. When Regina captured me, there were no automobiles. She is *here*. And she has found another victim.

Turning around quickly is a mistake. The lights, blaring music, and at least a dozen shots of rum conspire against me, and I start to fall, nearly taking a small pack of female wolves to the ground with me.

Two of them shove me away as I hear Regina again. "Do not protest, dear. No talking now at all. Off we go."

"Stop!" My strained cry does not carry over the din, and when I get to my feet, I cannot see anything but a mass of people waiting to enter the club for its after-midnight soiree. "Get out of my way," I snarl, but all I am is a drunk asshole, and no one listens.

"Regina!" I call at the top of my lungs. "Regina, you fucking bitch, stop right now!"

But when I finally stumble into the street, there are only empty sidewalks and thick fog rolling in off of the bay.

Zoe

A pounding headache wakes me, and I groan as I sit up and rub my eyes. But the sound only gets louder. The walls are shaking. Someone's knocking. I stumble to my door and check the peephole.

Shit.

"Sin? How the hell did you find me?"

His eyes are bloodshot and very blue, and he smells like he took a bath in a bottle of rum and—ew—vomit.

"Regiiiinnnnaaa," he mumbles. "Nnnneeeddd…"

I step aside to let him stumble into my apartment, and as I shut the door, he tries to turn, but his legs tangle and he falls over.

"You're drunk off your ass." Tugging at his arm, I try to pull him up, but he's solid and apparently determined to stay on the floor. "And a mess. There's no way I'm letting you on my furniture like this."

I can't believe I'm doing this, but I kneel next to him and start peeling his jacket from his shoulders. "Off with this."

"Youuuuu…rrrrr….otherrrrr." He's staring at me like I'm a ghost, or worse, but he lets me prop him up to sitting.

"I'm not, and I'd appreciate it if you'd stop insisting I am." The jacket lands in a heap next to him, and I go to work on his black shirt. Stupid asshole. How dare he show up like this and make me take care of him after what he did to me this afternoon.

"Like…her…" Sin reaches up and tries to touch my cheek,

but I bat his hand away and finish with the last few buttons on his shirt.

"Holy fucking shit." His sculpted chest and abs are impressive, but they're also covered with scars. Long, thin lines, those same awful T shapes at the ends. Scooting around him, I have to swallow the horror sticking in my throat.

His back is even worse with at least twice the number of scars I saw on Temple's autopsy photo. How could one man—even if he is a demon—withstand so much pain?

"Sin, my God."

"God knows." The words escape on a whisper, and his head lolls forward. When I reach for his belt, he says, "Please. No."

I rest my hand over his heart and wait for him to look up at me. "You reek, and I'm pretty sure you can't stand on your own. But I'm going to get a blanket to cover you up. Stay here and don't try to move." I leave him with his arms around his knees, swaying slightly, and rummage around in my closet.

Once the blanket's draped over his body, I kneel back down and touch his cheek. "Give me your pants, and I'll throw everything in the wash. You can sleep this off on the couch. Okay? I'm so mad at you I should just leave you on the floor, but my grandmother would come back to haunt me if I did that."

"Mad's....not here. You are. How?"

He's not making any sense. My patience is long gone, but so is Sin's fight, and when I reach for his belt this time, he doesn't protest. The blanket covers most of what he very obviously doesn't want me to see, but the brief glimpse I catch of his right thigh reveals more scars—burns this time.

It takes us ten minutes to traverse the few feet to the couch, Sin crawling on his knees with me bracing him so he doesn't fall over, but once he's stretched out under the blanket, he forces his eyes open and for one second, I think he actually focuses on me. "Thank you, Zoe."

"Yeah, well...you might not feel the same way in the morning with the hangover you're definitely going to have. Good night, Sin."

ELEVEN

Sin

The scent of coffee rouses me. I force my eyes open and wince against the bright lights. Fuck. It has been years since I had a hangover this terrible. Worse, I can feel the first stirrings of hunger in my gut. Soon, I will need to find a willing snack.

"I wouldn't get up if I were you."

Zoe. The last hour of my night comes screaming back to me in a rush. Searching for Regina. Failing to find her. Stopping at a liquor store for a bottle of Absinthe and using it to dull the pain of my memories.

Then...ending up here.

She sets a mug of coffee down on the end table. "You're naked under there, and I don't fancy a show."

From the way her cheeks tinge pink, she does. Very much. But I, on the other hand, do not want to give her one. This was —is—inappropriate on every level.

Drawing the blanket closer to my chest, I sit up and groan. "I owe you an apology."

"Several."

With a sigh, Zoe leans against the arm of a chair a few feet away. She wears a long, peach robe, and her red curls are damp. Her scent wraps around me—coconut and watermelon—and I breathe deeply, wanting more. I do not understand why her mere presence both soothes and irritates me, but under the blanket, my cock rises to attention, and I shift my legs to hide my reaction from her.

"Several, then. Was I...indelicate? Indecent?" The way my body is reacting to her now is definitely the latter, but hopefully she has not noticed. I bow my head, letting the rich scent of coffee replace all else, and the first sip eases the pounding behind my eyes.

"No. But you woke me well after midnight, stumbled in here babbling and smelling of puke, and then passed out. Plus, you left me at headquarters yesterday with no explanation. Alone. On *my first day*."

She keeps her tone soft, thankfully, but the judgment is clear. She believes me to be an asshole. She would be right. I am.

"It was a difficult evening."

"No shit." Draining her mug, she sets it in the kitchen sink. "Your clothes are clean and hanging on the back of the bath-room door. I'm going to get dressed. There's a spare toothbrush on the sink. Towels are in the linen closet. Shower. Use anything you need of mine—I don't like girlie scents, so you won't end up smelling like a flower shop—and then, assuming you weren't a total and complete idiot and left your car wher-ever you were drinking, I'll drive you to go pick it up."

As she scoots past me, I reach out and grab her wrist. "Zoe?" She doesn't pull away, but her shoulders stiffen and she holds her breath. "I am sorry. You deserve a better partner. If you wish, I will speak to Commander Eve."

Her gaze softens slightly. "We both know that's not going to happen. This is my case now just as much as it is yours. So you're going to pull yourself out of your current pity-party-bender and start being honest with me. What I *deserve*—what I want—is for *you* to be a better partner. To help me rather than standing in my way. So get on that."

With a little huff, she twists free of my hold, and when the bedroom door closes with a soft click, I nod. She is right. I need to be better, and I will. Because while most of the previous night is a blur, I do remember one thing very clearly.

Regina is no longer in Hell, and I fear she just kidnapped another shifter.

Zoe

Longest. Night. Ever. Lying awake as I tried to forget the sight of my partner's mostly naked body? Torture. Listening to him scream at 3:00 a.m.? So much worse. I don't think he remembers the nightmare. Or how I rushed out in just my sleep tank and skimpy shorts and tried to wake him. Or how he grabbed me and held on like his life depended on it for all of a minute before passing out again. Or the words he kept repeating over and over again.

"*I failed you. Lost you.*"

Failed me? Sure, he was an ass. And a shitty partner. But the anguish in his words was so much more than leaving me alone on my first day would ever warrant. And he certainly didn't lose me. Was he talking about someone else?

I should tell him about the nightmare. Better to come clean now than have him remember in a week, right? Making a mental note to ask Kunchin to tell me more about incubi, I pull on a pair of jeans and a black sweater. Everything else in my wardrobe hangs off me these days, but these two pieces? They're from my time at the police academy when I was running five miles a day, and they're about the only clothes I own that make me feel...good. Maybe even sexy.

Stop it, Zoe. He's your partner. And he's a demon. Just because he needed you in the middle of the night doesn't mean anything can or will happen. In fact, you need to make sure it doesn't.

Except when Sin emerges from the bathroom fully dressed, his black hair tamed, and stubble covering his jaw, his eyes hold a heat I know wasn't there yesterday.

"You look better," I say, a little surprised at how quickly he bounced back from what had to be one hell of a hangover.

"I feel like shit. But I will live. We should go." He picks up his phone from the coffee table where I set it the previous night and glances at the screen, then frowns. "My car is parked a block from a shifter club called Loup Noir, and we need their security footage."

"Why?" I grab my keys, crossbody bag, and travel mug. Sin looks back at the coffee pot longingly, and I arch a brow as I point to the insulated cup's twin sitting on the counter. "Take it. I'm mad, not a heartless bitch."

His laugh surprises me, and from his expression, it might surprise him too. "A heartless bitch would not have let me in last night."

"You didn't give me much choice. Pretty sure you would have passed out in the hall. That would have earned me a stern lecture from the building manager, and I'm already on his shit list."

Sin keeps pace with me as I take the stairs three floors down to the underground parking garage. "Why are you 'on his shit list'?"

I sink into the well-worn driver's seat and start the car, then grip the steering wheel so tightly, two of my knuckles crack. "After Temple..." Swallowing the lump in my throat, I force myself to take a deep breath. "I lost it for a while. Only I didn't have anywhere else to go, so instead of crashing at a partner's place, I puked in the mail room. Twice."

"We will stop them," Sin says quietly. "I promise."

LOUP NOIR DOESN'T LOOK like much from the outside. Not at 9:00 a.m. in the morning, anyway. A massive steel door, no windows, and the usual complement of detritus scattered over the sidewalk. The only indication it's a club at all? The plastic wrist bands in the gutter. "You spent your night *here*? No wonder you smelled like death."

The sound Sin makes is something close to a growl. "This is one of the more reputable clubs in the city. Like the members themselves, the exterior transforms when it opens."

He doesn't even glance at his car before going up to the door and pressing a small, almost invisible button at eye level.

"We don't open until seven," a weary voice says through an overhead speaker.

"Agents Sinclair and Dawes from the Bureau. We need to speak to Jinx immediately."

"Jinx?" I mouth.

Sin takes my arm and draws me away from the door a few feet. "You are about to enter a world unlike anything you have seen before. Let me take the lead, and above all, do *not* stare."

"I spent all of yesterday afternoon with a *Yeti*," I hiss. "If I can get through that, I can—"

The door opens, and the woman beckoning us inside is so stunning—and so very *other*—that my jaw drops open.

Sin elbows me in the side as he steps in front of me. "Dion. I did not expect to see you here this early."

"Look who's talking," the—what? Panther?—says as she holds the door open for us. "You were pretty wasted when you stumbled out of here."

"That is putting it mildly. My partner, Agent Zoe Dawes. This is her second day with the Bureau, so I hope you will forgive her for being less than...discreet." His words hold so much disdain, I want to take that travel mug and smack him upside the head.

"Honey," Dion coos as she wraps one very sleek, furry arm around my shoulders, "your partner's an ass. You're human?"

"Yes." I'm not quite sure how to feel about her motherly tone, or the way she steers me to the bar and pulls out a stool.

"Then today only, you're allowed to ask one question about me, panthers, shifters in general... Any question. No judgment." Her smile shows no evidence of feline teeth, and her golden eyes hold both exhaustion and amusement.

"I thought shifters would either look fully human or fully...animals."

Her fur ripples and fades away, leaving the most beautiful bronzed skin without a single blemish, though she shivers and goosebumps rise on her bare arms. Running a hand over sleek, black locks that tumble over her shoulders and over her green tank, she says, "Does this make you more comfortable?"

Frowning, I shake my head. "No. That's not what I meant. No one has the right to ask you to look or act or *be* someone you're not. My comfort isn't the issue—nor did it bother me to see you as you were. Shit. You're gorgeous in both forms. But all the books with shifters, at least, talk about them changing from one form to the other. I never thought you could hang out somewhere in between."

A decidedly feline purr starts low in her chest as fur covers her skin once more, and her amber eyes change shape subtly, angling out at the corners as her nose flattens. "I like you, Agent Zoe Dawes. I think we're going to be friends. The jury's still out on your partner, though. Short answer? When I look like this, I feel more...powerful. More me. Plus, fur does a better job regulating my temperature than my naked skin does."

"This is all new to me," I say with my first genuine smile of the day. "Thank you."

Dion swipes a rag over the bar and glances down at her phone. "Jinx is gonna be a few minutes. Can I get you a refill on those coffees?"

Clearly, I need to work on my poker face, because as soon as my smile falls away, Dion leans forward and lowers her voice. "Hon, these are Blue Bottle beans. We only serve the cheap shit at night. When it's just me and Jinx here, we spring for the good stuff."

This is the most comfortable I've felt since I started at the Bureau, and I slide a hip onto the stool and pop the lid on my mug. "It was a long night. I'd love another cup."

"Not as long as his," Dion says as she tops off Sin's mug as well. "Next time, demon, you're cut off after the fifth drink."

My brows shoot up. "Fifth? How much did you have last night, Sin?"

He remains silent and sullen, but Dion snorts. "Bastian kicked him out after number twelve."

"You did six shots of vodka right in front of me, one after another," Sin mutters.

"And I burn it off in no time." Dion slaps her ass, clad in tight hot pants, and then winks at me. "Best part of being born this way? The metabolism. When my cousin got married last year, I went camping down in Yosemite. Spent three nights runnin' from sundown to sunup. Came back fifteen pounds lighter. Though it works both ways. My grocery bill's through the roof."

After another sip of coffee, I meet her gaze. "Can I ask one more question?"

Dion's easy to talk to, and Sin definitely isn't. When she nods, I give him a pointed look, and he mutters something that might be "*Humans,*" before wandering over to the railing that looks down onto a dance floor.

"What's the one thing you wish humans knew about shifters? Or the biggest misconception we have."

"We are *definitely* going to be friends, hon." Resting her elbow on the bar, she fiddles with the strap of her tank for a moment. "That we're really no different than you are. Most of those in the *Other* community are just like the friends and family you've known your whole life. Hell, a bunch of them *are* your friends and family, they've just never come out to you. We want the same things. Solid relationships, trust, love, respect. That's why losing Jacinda hurts so much. And why your partner saw me pound the vodka." Dion's eyes water, and she swipes the back of her hand over her cheek. "That girl was the sweetest thing."

It takes me a moment to put the pieces together, and when I do, I glare at Sin. "Seriously? When were you going to tell me you got a name?"

He flinches. "When I sobered up enough to remember I hadn't."

If so many of my nights recently hadn't ended at the bottom of a bottle of Jack, I'd be harder on him for his actions. But the hell I went through only left me with one scar. His? I think it almost destroyed him.

TWELVE

Jinx beckons us from the back office, and as I follow behind Zoe, I kick myself, yet again, for letting my past interfere with this case. If I had been sober last night, perhaps I could have stopped Regina. Or trailed her to find Thorn—and the missing shifters.

The very idea of seeing Thorn again, of hearing his voice, of the mere *chance* he could snare me in his inescapable thrall a second time... I stifle a shudder. In Hell, I endured centuries of torture. By the end, madness had consumed me. And yet, my time in the Underworld was nothing compared to what Thorn did to me.

"Sin?" Zoe whispers. "Are you all right?"

I shoot her a look warning her to keep quiet, and she rolls her eyes. I deserved that.

"Agent Dawes and Agent Sinclair," Jinx says as she drops lightly into her chair and taps a few keys on her keyboard. "Dion says you need to review our security footage."

I blow out a slow breath. "When I was leaving last night, I heard a woman convincing one of your patrons to go with her. I believe this woman is a person of interest in our case. Perhaps even the murderer's accomplice."

Jinx presses her hand to her chest. "You think this same woman took Jacinda?"

Glancing over at Zoe, I see the accusation in her green eyes. She's learning just how much of an ass I am. Particularly when drunk. "I do. We cannot go into detail—not with an open investigation—but what happened to Jacinda has happened before. If this woman is using your club as a poaching ground, we might be able to set a trap for her and put an end to this for good."

With a curt nod, Jinx brings up a screen showing six different video images. "If your suspect is using *my* club to hunt, she will regret ever being born. We protect our own, Sinclair. Not that we won't accept the Bureau's help, but if this woman shows up on video and we *ever* see her again, I will intervene and stop her."

"Jinx, I'm new to the Bureau." Zoe sits up a little straighter in her chair, an earnest look on her face. "But I was with the SFPD for six years. I promise you...if you let us handle this, we *will* find this woman—and anyone else she's working with—and we'll stop them."

"Dion likes you, human." Jinx inclines her head as if she's doubting her manager's word. "But I do not know you, and there is something about you that's—"

"Jinx," I say sharply. "The only one allowed to insult my partner in my presence is *me*. And we require privacy. Give us the room, and you can view the feeds later at your leisure."

Zoe shoots me a look that could flay my skin from my body, but as that particular torture is one I've survived multiple times, I shake it off. It is better if she does not know anything about her *Other* side—whatever it may be. If she were to discover it, or use any talents she might have, she could be even more of a target than she is already. Thorn would hunt her down and invade her mind until he wrung every last drop of power from her soul. And then, he would drive her slowly, painfully insane.

I do not know how to tell her that her mere association with me puts her in danger. I did not see Regina the previous night, and I do not believe she saw me. But if I am wrong?

Fuck. I should never have gone to Zoe's apartment. I could have been followed. Commander Eve needs to assign Zoe a security detail.

"Get your head in the game, Sin," Zoe snaps as she starts the video playback. "I don't know where you keep going, but it isn't here with me."

I draw in a sharp breath. There are times that the woman at my side seems so familiar. And very much...*mine*, that she takes my breath away. The look on her face now? It stirs emotions in me I have never felt before. I cannot let myself give in. Emotion —*any* emotion—is a danger to both of us.

It takes me only seconds to get myself under control. After all, I have had years of practice feeling...nothing. "Apologies. It will not happen again."

"I hope not."

The images on the screen pass by at double speed, starting half an hour before midnight. I cringe as one of the feeds captures me stumbling through the crowd on my way to the door. My footsteps are uneven, my shoulders slump, and I am clearly belligerent.

"No more investigating on your own," Zoe snaps. "I can't believe you. Even when I was at my lowest, I never—*never*—drank on the job, and I don't care what time it was. You were clearly on the job."

"No one knows my faults better than me. I do not need you

to remind me of them at every turn." My anger is so bright and hot, I almost miss the glimpse of long, black hair against deathly pale skin. Or the flash of orange in her eyes. "There. That is Regina." Jabbing the keyboard, I slow the video to normal speed and rewind to play it a second time.

"Look at the girl next to her," Zoe says, pointing to a small, frizzy-haired shifter. "I saw her on the video earlier. She's been at the club for at least an hour, and she's following Regina around like a little lost puppy dog."

"Do *not* let any of the shifters hear you compare them to puppies." That is the last thing we need.

"Pay attention." Zoe grabs the mouse and starts zooming in on Regina and her target. The demon traces her finger down the shifter's cheek, and the girl smiles, her eyes blank, and nods. "Dammit. I wish we had sound."

"We do not need it. Regina is Fae, and with her particular power, she can cast a charm with an effect similar to Rohypnal using only her words. There is no fighting it. Not even the strongest mind can break free. Her victim will be compliant, dazed, and do whatever Regina asks. When the charm wears off, she will likely remember nothing."

"Shit."

I can feel Zoe's horror, but it is nothing compared to my own. For Regina's charms did not work as well on me as she'd thought. I was too strong, and though I could not fight her, I was often semi-aware of what she was making me do. The longer we spend working this case, the more I remember how she *prepared* me for Thorn's torture. And how he stole everything I was, slowly, painfully, until I finally broke completely.

We watch together as the shifter follows Regina out the club's front door without saying a word, passing within ten feet of me. I'd fallen, facing away from them. Minutes later, I believe I vomited in the gutter. Had I been sober, I would have found her, and perhaps, the pretty young shifter with the frizzy hair and bright, blue eyes would still be free today.

Zoe

Back at Bureau headquarters, we stand in front of Commander Eve, Sin staring straight ahead, focused on something over her shoulder as he recounts his drunken night and how close he was to Regina.

Halfway through Eve's tirade dressing down for his stupidity, I clear my throat. "Commander?"

"Yes, Agent Dawes? Please do not tell me you condone this behavior." Her pupils are pinpricks of onyx, and she's angry enough, her fingernails take on a decidedly talon-like appearance, but her voice is still calm—too calm, in fact—that scary type of calm that warns how close to the edge she is.

"No, Commander. Of course not. But I've had my share. You were watching me after Temple's death. You know I didn't handle that particularly...well."

Sin may have been an idiot, but every person—or demon—on the planet has made mistakes. Some of them legion. The longer she takes to rip him a new one, the more time we lose. The shifter's been gone for almost twelve hours now, and we still don't know her name.

Eve jerks out of her chair and marches over to Sin. The tall, blond eagle shifter jams her hands onto her hips and stares up at him. "You had better get your head on straight, Sinclair. Regina doesn't get to use my city as her new hunting grounds, and Thorn is not going to leave San Francisco alive. Understand?"

He nods, still not meeting her gaze.

"Get out of here. Both of you," she snaps.

Gathering the photos we'd printed from the security feeds, I tuck them into my bag as I follow Sin to our desks. "Give me the best picture we have," he says as he logs in to his computer. "I will show you how to release an official APB for a person of interest."

With my chair next to his, I watch him go through the various steps. There's a heaviness to his movements, a resignation, an exhaustion, like every key weighs ten pounds. I can't help staring at Regina's photo. Her frame is almost skeletal, and something about her orange eyes leaves a vague sense of dread in the pit of my stomach.

"Take over," Sin mutters as he pushes up and starts to pace in a circle around our desks. "After her description, add the following: Suspect is extremely dangerous, and can compel anyone with her voice. If seen, do not approach without ear protection. She has millennia of experience hiding in the shadows and blending in, and should be considered one of the most dangerous criminals the Bureau has ever sought. Contact Agents Sinclair and Dawes with any potential sightings immediately."

"Damn, Sin. Isn't that a little...overkill?" I shut my mouth when I see the look on his face. Nope. Apparently it's not. I save Regina's description and push back from his desk. "What do we use for facial recognition here?"

"The Global Habitant Optical Scanning and Tracking system," he says, leaning over me to tap the touchscreen.

"What the hell kind of name is that?" As I focus on the icon, I realize why it sounds so...ridiculous. "Really? The GHOST system? At BOO. How do we expect anyone to take us seriously when we have acronyms like that?"

Sin arches a brow. "Agent Dawes, that is exactly the point. We do not want the general public knowing about us, and if they were ever to hear about the Bureau and our systems, the more ridiculous they think the names are, the better."

"Why do we care? We have Mem-Clear. If we find someone who's not ready to know about us, we can just—"

"No." The word escapes on a snarl, and Sin slams his hand down on his desk, making the keyboard clatter and several other agents stare at us and whisper amongst themselves. "We do *not* deploy Mem-Clear like it is candy."

Kunchin strides over, his massive, furry frame so tall, I have to crane my neck to see his face. "Everything okay here, Zoe?"

"Fine," I say with a forced smile. "My partner's got a giant stick up his ass, though." Sin glares at me, but says nothing. "I don't suppose you could show me how to use the GHOST system?"

"Sure." The yeti gives my chair a gentle push and crouches down next to me. His large hands dwarf the keyboard, but he can type faster than anyone I've ever seen. "Just enter all known visual information here, then click source image and find the digital file you want to match."

"That one." I point to the one clear image we were able to gather off Loup Noir's security feeds.

"Gotcha." Kunchin selects the photo, and after it uploads, he points to the big red button at the bottom of the screen. "Go for it."

I'm practically grinning as I click the *Match* button. It's silly. I've done this same thing hundreds of times for the SFPD, but this feels...so much more important. Heavier. Like I've finally discovered my purpose in life.

With a nod, Kunchin pats my forearm. "Good job, rookie." As he shoulders Sin to one side, he mutters, "Cut her some slack."

At least someone around here is nice. And normal. Well, other than the thick white fur and long, sharp canines that perch on his gray lower lip. How the hell does he manage to go outside and not get noticed?

"He uses a perception filter," Sin says quietly.

Springing to my feet, I whirl around and get right in his face. "Were you just using your *talents* on me?"

He offers me a dry chuckle. "Your expression gave your thoughts away, Zoe." Sobering, he pins me with that deep blue stare that seems to see right into the depths of my soul. "I swore to you that I would never feed from you—or use my talents on you—without your knowledge, and I do not break my promises."

"Everyone breaks promises," I say, fighting a sudden, unexpected, and completely illogical urge to burst into tears.

Sin digs his fingers into his left forearm, then grimaces in pain. "I suppose they do. The last time I failed to keep my word, I lost everything. I will not do so again. You can trust me, Zoe."

I want to. With everything I am. But if I do, and he betrays me? I'll never trust anyone again.

"Come with me. Facial recognition will take at least an hour or two. We can set up in a conference room again and start investigating the one shifter we *have* managed to identify." When I hesitate, he sighs. "I will buy lunch. Will you join me?"

"Fine." I grab my satchel and follow him upstairs.

When we're set up in the same room he ran out of yesterday, he meets my gaze. "What do you eat?"

"Um, food."

Sin rolls his eyes. "My knowledge of humans is not *that* limited. Sandwiches? Tacos? Pad Thai? The Bureau has accounts at a handful of local restaurants, and there is a taco truck not too far from here."

"I'm always up for tacos. What do *you* eat? Besides arousal." This is as close to an honest conversation as we've had since I started, and though it's superficial and silly, I need to find some way to connect with him or this is never going to work.

"I enjoy tacos." The corner of his mouth turns up in what might be considered a smile—in some other fucked up universe —and he logs in to the Bureau's computer system to pull up our case notes. "The truck I am particularly fond of opens in two hours. Shall we see what we can find on Jacinda while we wait?"

"Sounds like a plan," I say, finally feeling a spark of hope that maybe this partnership won't go down in flames.

THIRTEEN

Across the conference room table, Zoe fiddles with a beaded bracelet she pulled off her right wrist an hour ago. It seems to calm her—this repetitive motion—and if I am honest, the quiet clicking of the beads helps me focus as well.

Something has changed between us since she defended me in front of the commander. Or perhaps it changed last night and I did not notice.

She sits back in her chair and peers up at the wall of computer screens. While I spent the previous night trying to dull the pain of my memories with alcohol, she pulled the records for every one of Thorn's suspected victims across the country.

The GHOST system is not only for facial recognition. It also runs advanced pattern matching algorithms, and as she stretches her arms over her head, it beeps, and the computer's melodious voice says, "Report Compiled. Would you like to hear the results?"

"Yes!" Zoe says, jumping up, bracing her hands on the table, and staring at the screens like they hold the answers to all the questions in the known universe. Her zeal is refreshing, and a bit infectious.

"Victims are shifters, witches, and Fae between the ages of twenty-two and thirty-five, with a median age of twenty-eight. All have either green or amber eyes, long hair, and no tattoos at the time of their abductions. All have verified credit card charges at supernatural bars or clubs in the week prior to their disappearance."

The computer displays the list of bars for every city, and I curse under my breath. Each city has at least three different establishments listed, some as many as five.

I run a hand through my hair, tugging at the short strands to help me focus. "That does not give us enough information to figure out if Regina is likely to return to Loup Noir or not." Meeting Zoe's gaze, I arch a brow. Time to see if she is confident in her own deductive reasoning. "What do your instincts tell you? Will she try somewhere else? Or stay with an establishment she knows?"

"You're more likely to be able to answer that than I am." With a frown, Zoe peers at another screen with a list of San Francisco's twenty-seven separate bars and clubs that cater to the *other*. "But whatever we decide, I think we should stick together." Her tone is firm, but her green eyes hold understanding without a hint of judgment.

"If we split up, we can cover more ground." The last thing I want is her investigating on her own, but nor do I want her to be seen with me. Of the establishments on the list, I count three Regina would never visit, including the poshest bar in the city, the Top of the Mark. If I sent Zoe there, she'd be safe, and I would be able to hunt. Alone.

She spreads her hands flat on the table between us and

arches a brow while pinning me with a hard stare. "No. Didn't you listen to the victim profile, Sin? Regina's looking for women exactly like me. Green eyes. Long hair. No tattoos. At bars that cater to the *other*. And I know what she looks like. I can help you trap her. And stop her from taking someone else."

Fuck.

"I know," I snap. "For the love of all that is holy in this world, Zoe, I *know*. Which is why I do not want you with me. You have no defenses against Regina, and if you are caught unawares, you could disappear before I would be able to stop her! I would never forgive myself if I lost you."

"If you *lost* me? Sin, you don't *have* me to lose. We're partners. Nothing more." Wariness infuses her tone, and her denial makes me want to punch something. Or wrap her in my arms.

I push up and start to pace the long, narrow conference room. "If Thorn has escaped Hell, everything he has done since that day is my fault."

"Why? You *sent* him to Hell, right? How is what happened afterwards in any way on you?" She rounds the table and, hands on her hips, stops right in front of me. "He's the bad guy. Well, so's Regina, but still. You were a victim. It's time you realize that."

"I. Helped. Them." I do not know how else to convey the depths of my guilt. I cannot tell her all the things I did under his influence. All the young women I tortured until they begged me to kill them. All the men I lured into the shadows so Regina could use her charms to compel them into obedience.

"You—"

The air in the room crackles, and I grab Zoe a split second before a blast of percussive energy shoves us both against the wall. Had I been any slower, her head would have hit the large computer screens, and unlike my own corporeal body, hers would have broken in several places.

"Sin?" Zoe's voice trembles, and she clutches my arms as she blinks hard to focus. "What just happened?"

"Agent Zoe Dawes," I say as I brush a thick, auburn curl away from her face. "You are about to meet your first archangel."

Zoe

Pressed against Sin's sculpted chest, I struggle to process his words. Archangel? My head hurts, like the world's worst pressure change just sucked all the brain matter from between my ears, and the air in the room feels somehow richer. Like there's more oxygen than there was a moment ago.

Sin steadies me, staring over my shoulder with such intensity, I'm worried he's about to lose his shit.

You can do this. Turn around. It's only one of God's chosen. No big deal, right?

When I manage to screw up enough courage to move, my tongue sticks to the roof of my mouth. The man—is he a man?—is beautiful. Long golden hair falls in gentle waves to his shoulders, and his skin glows as if dusted with silver and gold. Wings fold against his back, pure white, and his robes move like there's a gentle breeze swirling around only him.

"Sinclair."

Shit. Even his voice is perfect. Smooth and low and with a hint of an accent I can't place.

"Gabriel. This is Zoe."

The angel turns his golden-eyed gaze to me and frowns. Even that doesn't mar his beauty. "Interesting," he says.

Interesting? An angel just materialized out of thin air, and all he has to say is "interesting"?

Sin still has an arm around my waist, and the reassuring weight and his warmth might be the only things keeping me standing.

"Well?" Sin demands. "Is Thorn still Lucifer's *guest*?"

"No." The archangel shakes his head softly and stares up at the ceiling. "And the Almighty is fucking pissed about it."

Hearing the *Angel Gabriel* swear is almost too much, and I lean a little more against Sin. "I need to sit down."

Almost immediately, my partner guides me over to a chair. "I can meet with him alone," he whispers close to my ear. "Rest."

"No. I want to hear this. All of it." He's bracing his hand on the table, close enough I can smell my soap on his skin. I can't believe I'm about to do this, but I look to Gabriel. "I realize you could probably smite me down or something for even asking, but could you give us a minute?"

I expect anger or even shock, but all I see on Gabriel's face is boredom. "I am an angel, Zoe Dawes. Even if I left the room, I could eavesdrop as simply as you breathe."

Sin turns my chair so I'm facing him. "What is it?"

"You haven't told me the whole story." Shame wells in his blue eyes, now streaked with hints of crimson, and I drape my fingers over his. "I'm human, Sin. I'll never be able to imagine what you went through. But without the details, I can't help catch these bastards. Whatever you're afraid of telling me? Is it that much worse than what these kidnapped men and women are going through right now?"

My partner shakes his head, the reddish cast to his irises deepening. "I should have done more."

This man—demon—I thought was a complete and total asshole isn't. Not really. He's damaged. Scared even. And unable to admit it to anyone. I suppose we both are. Perhaps

Commander Eve knew what she was doing when she put us together.

I tighten my hold, and he shifts very subtly closer to me. Something about the action screams for me to reassure him. "Hey. You can do more *now*. By letting me in. When Gabriel leaves, you're buying me lunch and we'll play a few rounds of 'you show me yours and I'll show you mine.'"

Sin's full lips twitch for a second until he gets his expression under control, and he nods. "I guarantee I will win every round, Zoe."

"I'm sure you will."

"If the two of you are about done?" Gabriel asks, his voice full of disdain, but still oddly addicting. Like he's a melody I could listen to over and over again. One I could swear I've heard before in my dreams. "I have spent most of one of your *days* down in Lucifer's den, and I need to rid myself of the stench.

I don't know what he's talking about. Gabriel smells like a summer's day. But I keep my mouth shut as Sin takes a seat next to me. "*Our* days?" he says. "You have spent too much time in the celestial realm. How are you supposed to serve as a spiritual guide to the devoted if you do not know anything about them?"

"I know enough," the angel mutters. "But that is not why I am here. Lucifer attempted to hide it, but in the end, he admitted the truth. Hell was breached."

"Breached? Hell?" My voice rises and cracks, and I'm pretty sure my eyes can't open any wider. "How the hell—shit. How the fuck did someone breach Hell?"

Gabriel sighs. "A vampire was kidnapped from this realm two years ago and spent many months being punished for crimes he did not commit. When he was rescued, the demon called Thorn and his concubine Regina…" he shakes his head, "I suppose the proper phrase would be 'hitched a ride.'"

"And no one noticed? What is the Devil doing with his time if not watching over those he is charged to punish for all eternity?" Sin's tone is strained, and he's gripping the arm of the chair hard enough I can hear the wood protest.

"Lucifer had…other concerns." Gabriel, now seated across from us with his wings awkwardly brushing the floor, rests his elbows on the table. "There are forces at work in this realm you know nothing about, Sinclair. Forces that could open the Gates of Hell permanently. Michael, Raphael, and I are going to meet with a small group attempting to stop the uprising, but that is all we know at this time."

"Fuck," Sin says sharply. "How many more will die…?"

Gabriel's face sobers, and his golden eyes turn almost black. "Millions. But that is why you must find these two and send them back where they belong." Before Sin can say another word, the angel holds up his hand. "You have paid your debt."

Pulling several sheets of folded paper from within his robes, Gabriel holds Sin's gaze. "The runes and sigils you will need to bind them and send them to the Underworld. As long as you follow the instructions, there is no danger you will be trapped with them."

"Give me one good reason why I should trust you," Sin mutters.

The betrayal in Sin's voice squeezes my heart in a vise, and though I've never considered myself a touchy-feely person, with him, I'm different. More…me somehow. So I do the only thing I can. Under the table, I briefly press my knee to his. A subtle gesture of support.

Gabriel rises and smoothes his hands down his robes. His wings flutter, stretching until they practically touch either side of the room. "We made many mistakes with your case, Sinclair. Some you know. Others...I am bound not to reveal. But Nathanial and I, at least, are in agreement. We have been for some time. Your debt was paid, even though I know you do not agree. Your exile to this realm could have ended years ago, but you chose to stay. If you trust nothing else, trust this. I am on your side."

With that cryptic statement, the angel turns to me. "Agent Zoe Dawes, there is something about you that does not add up. Something...*other*. I am not certain what it is, but still, I wish you luck with Sinclair. He can be a handful, but he is a good man."

Before I can respond, what feels like a percussion grenade pressurizes the entire room. My heart hammers against my chest, and I'm so dizzy, I want to throw up. I can't move until Sin pulls me against him, his fingers threading through my hair and his lips brushing my ear. "Just breathe, Zoe. I have you now."

FOURTEEN

Zoe is shaken after Gabriel's visit, and the memories the archangel stirred in me leave me desperate to see the sun. "You will feel better after you eat something," I say as I save our research and shut down the conference room computers.

"I'll feel better when shit like that stops surprising me," she mutters and pinches the bridge of her nose. "Damn. I don't suppose there's any aspirin in this place?"

I can sense her pain, and though I do not think she will allow it, I am capable of taking it away. "My talents can help. Will you trust me?" Offering her my hand, I wait, and after a beat, she nods, but the look in her eyes is anything but certain.

"What would you have to do?"

"I can attempt to convince your mind to ignore the pain. Gabriel's presence triggered something very similar to what you call a migraine. It will pass in a few hours, perhaps a day at most."

Zoe chews on her lower lip. "You'd be manipulating my thoughts."

"Not exactly. Your autonomic nervous system only. Not your mind."

She needs more reassurance. We have been partnered less than forty-eight hours, and though Gabriel confirmed my belief that there is something *other* about her, we are very different. She is the Bureau's first human agent. Or, at least the first to make it through more than a single hour. The poor male first recruited has been in a mental institution for a decade now.

"I hold very little in this life dear, Zoe. My brother. My freedom. I swear on both of them, I will only ease your pain."

"Okay. But if I find out you tried to hypnotize me into clucking like a chicken, I *will* find a way to murder you," she says as she gives me her hand.

"I would expect nothing less." Releasing the tight control I keep on my abilities, I hold Zoe's gaze and let my mind seek out the source of her discomfort. Given enough time and strength, I could cure her migraine completely, but masking the symptoms so she can heal on her own will not drain much of my energy. Though by tomorrow, I will be forced to seek out several willing *donors*.

"Oh." Zoe sighs as I convince her mind the pain is gone. "That's amazing."

I wish I could tell her my true nature. That the relief she's feeling now does not come from my incubus talents, but from divine influence. Trust takes time, and if we are to find Thorn and Regina, I cannot risk fracturing what small amount we have built with honesty.

Breaking our connection leaves me with a distinct sense of loss and an emptiness that threatens to consume me. Fuck. I did not mean to let myself feel...*anything* for Zoe. Not sympathy. Not understanding. Not respect. Yet, all of those emotions and more run through me, and I push back so quickly, the chair almost topples over. "Meet me downstairs in five minutes," I say, keeping my tone as firm and professional as I can. "One of the best taco trucks in the city is on the way to Jacinda's apartment. We will stop for food first."

A pang of guilt hits me as I cross the threshold. Blindsiding her with our other task today would only destroy her appetite, and she has lost too much weight since her human partner's death. I hope to all that is holy she is strong enough to handle what comes next.

***

Zoe

Tacos El Primo doesn't look like much. A handful of dents on the front bumpers, scuffed white paint with splotches of bright pink, red, green, and blue, and a canopy that's seen better days. The menu only has four main items on it. Tacos, tortas, mulitas, and a ceviche bowl. Along with the normal accompaniments.

When we have our food—four tacos for me, two for Sin—we sit side by side on concrete benches overlooking the bay. "That's not much food," I say with a nod at Sin's plate.

"I do not technically *require* food." The look on his face as he takes a bite of his carne asada taco is like a kid in a candy store. "I simply enjoy it."

For a split second, I wish I were more like Sin. That I could enjoy things with the zeal I see in others. And then I take a bite. "Mother...*fucker*," I say through a mouthful of tortilla, shredded chicken, and salsa. "This is amazing."

Pride shines in his eyes, and he sits up a little straighter. "I have tried every truck in the city. None of them compare to this."

"That's dedication I can respect." I elbow him gently, but his expression sobers. "What?"

"I spent many centuries deprived of food," he says quietly. "Now, I choose my meals carefully. All of them."

"Tell me."

"You do not truly wish to know." He takes a sip from his bottle of Coke—the kind with real sugar—and shivers slightly.

"Maybe not. But I think I *need* to know." I take another bite, then pull up the hem of my sweater to reveal the two-inch scar from Temple's bullet. "I spent a week in the hospital. As far as gunshots go, it was pretty...average, I guess. No major organs hit, the wound was a through-and-through. Couple of rounds of antibiotics, fluids, rest...I was supposed to be good as new."

"Supposed to be?" Sin turns slightly, appraising me with a discerning stare. "Are you physically compromised? Do I need to worry?"

My cheeks heat, and I stare down at my plate of half-finished tacos. "No. It's nothing like that. It just...it still hurts. The department shrink says it's all in my head. I need to 'process my emotions' and 'honor my truth.' Shit like that."

Sin rests his fingers over the scar. His touch is almost electric, and my skin tingles in a familiar and very pleasant way. And then his lips curve into a frown. "No. This has nothing to do with any psychological trauma."

"Then what is it? Is it dangerous? What can I do about it?" A thousand possibilities run through my head in under thirty seconds. Am I dying? Did Temple *do* something to me?

"I am not certain." He gently eases my sweater down and turns to watch the waves breaking against the rocky shore. "You are not in any immediate danger from the injury, Zoe. What I am sensing is...strange. An energy I believe I have felt before, long ago. It may have something to do with Thorn's influence over your late partner. If my fucking memory were only intact..."

I nudge his plate closer to him. "Hey. You've done more for me in five minutes than my doctors and shrink did in three weeks. Eat. Let's go to Jacinda's, and after that, find somewhere we can talk. I know you don't want to relive what happened to you, but I think—"

"I need to." With a sigh, he picks up the greasy paper plate and stares at it like it's a serving of mashed peas drizzled with motor oil. But after a minute, he shakes his head, sighs, and picks up his remaining taco.

We finish our meals in silence, and I hope we'll come out of this case okay—or something okay-adjacent, at least. Because the way things seem now?

I'm terrified these murders—these demons—will be the end of us both.

JACINDA'S STUDIO APARTMENT in the Tenderloin is old and worn down, but nearly spotless. Even the threadbare furniture is pristine. Multi-colored votive candles in small Mason jars line every window sill, and though most everything in her refrigerator has expired—the milk a full week ago—even her shelves are organized.

"She was so young," I say as I examine a picture of her with Dion taken by the water on a sunny day. "Twenty-four, was it?"

"Yes." Sin rifles through her nightstand drawer. "Nothing of any note in here. No diary or journal, no sex toys. Only a bottle of Ambien, two highlighters, and this." He holds up a book with a photo of the Golden Gate on it. *The Local's Guide to San Francisco Living.*

"She'd only been here six months or so." I crouch next to a

small filing cabinet and give the handle a tug. Locked. "Don't suppose you found a key in there, did you?"

When Sin shakes his head, I pull a small, zippered pouch from my bag and go to work on the lock. I could probably break the damn thing faster by just jamming a screwdriver between the drawer and the frame, but something about desecrating a victim's belongings has never sat well with me.

"You need to work on your speed," Sin says, coming up behind me. "And your technique." Kneeling, he slides his fingers over mine. "Your dominant hand will have better control, so let your other sense the movement of the tumblers. A lock this size probably has three. No more than four. Which one is loosest?"

I close my eyes, trying to ignore the feel of his body against mine, and probe the tiny lock carefully. "The back one."

"Good. Now find the next."

Despite practicing my skills for years, his simple piece of advice has me flying through the lock in under fifteen seconds.

"You learn quickly," he says, taking what feels like way longer than necessary—but less time than I'd like—removing his hands. Before I can slide the drawer open, he's halfway across the room, leaning against the wall. "I am afraid I judged you without cause yesterday. When we met. I was angry at the commander and did not want a new partner. Particularly one with no knowledge of our world."

"I was kind of surprised you could walk with that extra large stick up your ass." Offering him a small smile, I pull a stack of papers and a cardboard box out of the file cabinet. "Is this your way of saying you want a do-over?"

"It is my way of apologizing. Or telling you I want to. I am sorry for misjudging you, Zoe. I will try not to let it happen again."

We spend a few minutes rifling through the papers, but

they're just mundane remnants of a young woman's life. Her birth certificate, social security card, and a few bank statements.

Sin opens the box, and suddenly, it's like all the air is sucked out of the room. My chest tightens, and panic floods me, chilling me to the core. There's no logical reason for my reaction. It's just a dried flower in a small lucite box. But when I finally manage to take a breath and look to Sin, he seems to be as affected as I am.

"Wh-what kind of flower is that?" I ask.

"An orange blossom." His voice holds a quiet reverence, and he lifts the small memento like it's the most precious thing in the world. "One of my last memories before Regina found me was of walking through the orange groves of Florence in springtime. The scent...it is—it was—like nothing you have ever imagined, Zoe. I always thought it smelled like...freedom."

FIFTEEN

Zoe

When I was partnered with Temple, I always drove. Grunt work, he used to say. To sit passively while Sin drives is...odd. And a little terrifying. He claims his reflexes are better than a human's, but that doesn't mean I want him taking curves on two wheels.

"Will you slow down? Please? You're making me dizzy." I crack the window, sucking in the fresh, salty air to try to settle my stomach as he weaves through some of San Francisco's less traveled streets. He hasn't said a word since we left Jacinda's apartment. Seeing that orange blossom affected both of us deeply, but he was so trapped in his own memories, I don't think he noticed my panic.

I'm not about to tell him. I can't explain it, after all. I have no emotional connection to orange blossoms. They're pretty. I like orange juice as much as the next person. But that's all the attachment I feel towards them.

As he's forced to stop at a red light and I get my bearings, a sinking feeling twists my stomach. "Sin, where are we going?"

"Commander Eve spoke with your former lieutenant. The death of James Temple is now the Bureau's to investigate."

Oh, shit.

After I got out of the hospital, I begged Sergeant Perkins for access to Temple's apartment, but he refused me. Every time. I thought I was ready, but I'm not.

"Zoe. Look at me." Sin's voice snaps me back to the present, and I blink hard as I realize we're parked a block away from Temple's building. I was mired in my own head for at least five full minutes. "Temple was the first to be taken—that we know of. If we can find out how, where, and when, perhaps we will be able to predict their next move. The human detectives who searched his apartment would not have known what to look for. We may find evidence they missed."

"I know. I can do this." Maybe I want to convince myself as much as Sin, because I'm out of the car before he even kills the engine.

Still, I hesitate at the building's secure, outer door, the spare key I never took out of my bag trembling in my hand. Until Sin reaches my side, and I can breathe again. He's not the partner I thought I'd have. Or want. But he's a lot less "asshole" and a lot more "damaged" than I gave him credit for yesterday. And his presence calms me.

"I owe you an apology too," I say as I hand him the key.

"Oh?"

The building smells like old plaster and lingering water damage. Temple's apartment is—was—on the third floor, and we climb the stairs together.

"You weren't the only one who judged too quickly yester-day. This isn't my world, and I have a fuckton to learn."

Sin stops outside Temple's door and turns to me. The reddish ring around his irises is getting larger, but it doesn't lessen the intensity of his stare. "This *is* your world, Zoe. There is something *other* about you. But even if you never discover exactly what it is, you are a Bureau agent now, and you belong here."

This may be the most he's said to me at one time without prompting, and it shouldn't affect me so dramatically, but standing outside my former partner's apartment, his words almost reduce me to tears.

The SFPD seal is still in place, and the ripping sound it makes as I open the door reverberates through the hall. Sin touches my shoulder. "I should enter first. My senses are more acute than yours. I may be able to detect if anyone *other* has been here."

"Knock yourself out."

"I have never understood that expression," Sin says.

"Honestly, neither have I."

He moves through the apartment carefully, and I stay well behind him, wondering if he was trying to tell me I smell. "In here," he calls, strain in his tone, and I hurry to catch up. He's kneeling in front of the small gun safe Temple kept in his closet. It's open and empty.

"What is it? Every cop I know has one of those. The detective in charge of the case would have drilled the lock."

My partner peers up at me, discomfort tightening his features. "Incubi are predators by nature. We evolved to scent fear and arousal, the two emotions we can feed on most easily. The area around this safe carries both in equal measure."

"Are you trying to tell me Temple had...a *gun fetish*?"

With an exasperated sigh, he shakes his head. "No. I am trying to tell you that Regina was here with your former partner and forced him to do *something* with the contents of the safe. Either retrieve an item or leave one behind. Check your tablet. The inventory from your former precinct should be in there."

Shit. The idea that Temple was in his apartment with that woman—that Fae bitch—gives me the creeps, and I shudder as I pull up the case files.

"Two boxes of ammunition, unopened. A copy of his will—the scanned document is attached—the title to his vehicle, and a hunting knife."

"He used his service weapon in the attack," Sin says as he pushes to his feet. "If he was taken when he was off duty, perhaps it was in the safe, and Regina forced him to retrieve it."

"Why?"

"Power." With one last glance around the small, spartan bedroom, Sin motions for me to precede him back into the living room. "Most in the Bureau do not carry guns. Our talents are our weapons. The mages use athames on occasion, but that is it. You—as our lone human—will likely be the only agent in the building most days with a firearm."

"Well, that makes me feel...inadequate," I mutter.

"It is not meant to." He eases the tablet from my hand and sets it on the counter, where he taps the screen to bring up the scanned copy of Temple's will. "Thorn and Regina are experts in psychological torture. Tell me this, Zoe. How would you feel if you were forced to use your gun to take an innocent life?"

My voice drops to a whisper. "It would destroy me."

"Exactly. This was part of their plan to torture him. Human minds are strong." Sin's expression softens, and he offers me a sad smile. "Perhaps stronger than any other crea-ture. They do not quietly or easily submit. Not for long. Regi-na's touch and voice can compel anyone for short periods of time. A few hours at most. Long enough to get them some-where...private. Somewhere she and Thorn can secure them and delve deep into their thoughts to find the one or two things their victims hold most dear. That is what they then use to...break them."

The threat of tears burns my eyes, and I swallow hard. "So they kidnapped Temple, then decided that forcing him to kill me with his own gun would be enough to break him completely?"

A shadow passes over Sin's features. "Or, that being used to take you, to capture you, torture you, and ready you for...*use* would be even better."

Fuck. Even when I realized I fit the basic profile of Thorn's victims, I didn't put the pieces together. Maybe I didn't want to. I have to sit down. Right now.

My legs buckle, and Sin scoops me up and deposits me on a barstool. "Take a deep breath, Zoe."

"I'm...I'm fine. I don't...it was just a shock, that's all." I wave him off, and he takes a seat next to me. "But Sin? I need you to tell me everything you remember about your time with them."

"No." He reaches for my tablet and brings up the SPD report, but I'm not going to let him off the hook that easily.

"You've been giving me half answers the entire time we've been on this case, and I'm sick of it. You don't think this is hard for me? Being here? My partner *shot* me. He was like a brother to me. One of the only people in the world I trusted implicitly, and he held a gun to my side and pulled the trigger."

"And that is supposed to compare to what they did to me?" he shouts, standing and starting to pace the room. "Being forced to go against everything I have *ever* believed in?"

"Oh for fuck's sake. No. But it's supposed to make you realize that this case isn't all about *you!* It's about the missing women. And men. The ones who are going through hell right now. A hell only *you* can understand." I'm shouting now too, and he stares at me like I've lost my shit. And maybe I have, but I don't care. "I need you to explain it to me. Because maybe—

just maybe—you'll remember something you think is completely inconsequential, but really...is the missing piece of the puzzle that could help us figure out where they'll strike next."

Sin's knuckles crack as he balls his hands into fists, and his skin takes on a bronzed glow—almost like there's some internal fire brewing inside him itching to escape.

"We don't have to like each other, *Sinclair*. But we're partners, and partners don't keep secrets."

He flinches, as if my words have finally gotten through whatever shield he's using to keep his pain deep inside. The glow surrounding him fades away, and he walks over to the window in the far corner of the living space and looks out over a small slice of the city half-obscured by the building next to us.

"Are you certain you wish to do this here?" he asks.

No. I'm not. But if he's willing to talk, I'm not taking a chance leaving will change his mind. "Yes. I am."

Sin

I cannot look at Zoe. Not when I tell her about what I've done. I fully expect her to go straight to Commander Eve and request reassignment. She will not quit the Bureau. She is too strong for that. But she will never be able to look me in the eyes again. Of that I am certain.

There is only a small bit of sky visible through James Temple's window, and I wonder how most inhabitants of this city do not go mad living in these tiny boxes with no way to see the sun. Then again, most of them did not spend two centuries in Hell where only Lucifer's flames broke up the endless darkness.

I need fresh air, so I snap off the window lock and raise the sash. "I was young. For...what I am. A hundred and twenty-three earthen years. My brother had not even been born yet. This realm was full of people to feed from, and I was not as discerning back then."

"So, you took from people without consent?" Zoe asks, a wary edge to her voice.

"No. Not that. Never that. Until...Thorn." I force a deep breath, searching for a hint of the sea, but all I find is the stench of the dumpsters in the alley below. "I told you I was in Italy at the time. Florence. Besides the orange groves, one of my last clear memories is watching Michelangelo put the finishing touches on his David."

"Holy shit," she whispers.

"Indeed. He was a true genius." I risk a glance over my shoulder, and her green eyes are wide, awe bringing a beauty to her features I never want her to lose. But she will, any moment now. Returning my gaze to the window, I run a hand through my hair, the memory of how I wore it back then—long enough to brush my shoulders—so at odds with the more modern cut I favor now. "There was much unrest in Florence then, but still, the people celebrated every chance they could. A crowd of drunken Italians provided ample opportunity to feed, and I was ravenous. I know I glamoured two women that evening, but left them both with their virtues intact, and happy memories of dancing in the streets with their friends."

"You can *do* that? Change someone's memories?" The stool rattles, but I do not turn to her.

"Yes."

For several moments, neither of us speak. This is a mistake, but now that I have started, I cannot stop. "I was...drunk. On sexual energy and wine, and I cut through an alley on the way to my rooms. This is where my memories fade. But I remember

Regina. Her voice. Her words. 'You are a strong one, incubus. Come closer.'" Shaking my head, I brace my hands on the window sill. "I knew I should not listen, but her voice was like a siren's song, pulling me closer, like a drug. So I went. She kissed me, and then my mind...it is like a thick fog obscured everything. I have vague memories of walking, of falling, of pain. When the haze lifted, I was underground in a cage so small, I could not stand."

Zoe inhales sharply, and I continue. "They left me there for so long, I was out of my mind with hunger and thirst. No food or water. No energy I could sense anywhere around me to restore my strength. When Thorn—*mio maestro,* he ordered me to call him—entered the room, I tried to glamour him, but his mind is stronger than any other demon—any other creature—in all the known realms. And I...was too weak to move."

I am no longer in San Francisco. My body and mind are trapped in Italy. Locked underground and at his mercy. "'You will be my greatest weapon,' he said as he dragged me out of the cage. 'Your mind and body belong to me, and you will obey.'"

With a shudder, I bow my head, as I did back then.

"I tried to protest, but he called for two others. Men he had trapped and already broken. They chained me to a wall. Naked. My arms and legs spread wide. Once he started whipping me, the memories are so fragmented..." The scarred flesh of my arm throbs, and I dig my fingers into the old injury, needing the pain to keep me focused. "I know he used me to lure dozens of women. Regina brought in most of them, but the few who resisted her? All mages, for some of them had warded themselves against all other magical energy. They were no match for me. He would starve me before he allowed me out of the cage or the chains he kept me in, then force himself into my thoughts for hours until I was nothing but his puppet."

"And after? After you...*helped* him capture his victims?" Zoe asks, her voice barely a whisper.

"I was the one who chained them so he could brand them. Who transported them to whatever location Thorn had chosen to allow others to come and torment his victims. I cleaned up their dead bodies when their minds broke entirely. And I am the one who failed to help so many who begged me to kill them."

I slam my hand against the sill, cracking the wood, then whirl around. "Are you satisfied now, Zoe? Because I could go on about the parts I remember. How they screamed while being branded. How they sobbed as Thorn invaded their thoughts. Do you want to know how it felt? Because I can tell you that as well."

Zoe strides over to me, shoulders thrown back, but her breath stutters in her chest. I expect anger. Horror. Disgust.

Instead, she wraps her arms around me. She's shaking, and I know I am the cause, but still, she offers comfort? All I want to do is lose myself in her embrace, but I do not deserve this, and I pull away. "What was that?" I ask.

"My way of reminding you that you don't have to solve this case alone." Her eyes shimmer with unshed tears, and she blinks hard before she returns to the counter and slides her tablet into her bag. "We should get out of here. I'd much rather go through the SFPD report somewhere I don't feel like Temple's ghost is watching me."

I arch a brow. "There are no ghosts here."

"There are for me."

SIXTEEN

Sin

The parking structure beneath this building is poorly lit, with too many blind corners for my liking. But Zoe believes Temple kept a storage unit in the far corner of this garage, and though she would prefer to be anywhere other than here, her sense of duty will not let her leave without seeing it.

"There is no mention of any storage unit on the SFPD inventory of his assets," I say, following her as she weaves among rows of cars. "Are you certain about this?"

"No. But Temple was the kind of guy to have a..." she gestures vaguely with her hand, "bug-out bag."

"A what?"

"A go bag. Money, a fake ID...secrets." Zoe shrugs. "And if he had one, he'd want me to destroy it."

I fail to see how this will help us, and after finding the orange blossom in Jacinda's file cabinet, I worry Thorn and Regina know I am searching for them. True coincidences are far fewer than humans believe. If this was a warning, Zoe and I are both in danger.

"There are fifty storage lockers here, Zoe. We do not have time to break into every one of them."

"We don't have to," she snaps and tosses a scathing glare over her shoulder. "It's this one." Yanking her lock picks from her bag, she goes to work on locker number three-two-four, but her movements are punctuated by anger and grief.

"Give me those." The closer we get to dusk, the less patience I can muster. If Regina follows the established schedule, she will not take another woman tonight. Or tomorrow. But she will be searching. She may even choose a victim and compel them to return the next night. And the night after that. A test of sorts.

Zoe curses as I snatch the lock picks away, but I sidestep her and have the door open in under ten seconds.

"There. Take what you need so we can get out of here."

"There's that stick again." Zoe shoves me aside and reaches for a black bag. "Be careful when you sit down, Sin. Pretty sure this one's big enough to rip you a new asshole."

My fury rises as I growl, and she stares at me, her lips parted slightly. "Your eyes are almost completely red. Are you okay?"

"Fuck. I need to feed. Soon."

Zoe takes two quick steps back, the satchel clutched to her chest like it could somehow protect her if I decided to make her my next meal.

"I promised you I would not take from you, and I do not care how hungry I am, I keep my promises," I retort. "But when I am in this state, I am—as you have aptly stated—an asshole."

"Oh." She relaxes slightly, nods, and turns, pointing to the stairwell in the corner that leads to the street. "Then let's get out of here so you can find a meal. But drop me at home first. I'm not sure I'm ready to watch you feed."

My response is lost to an explosion that rocks the asphalt under our feet. Bits of stone rain down around us, and a dull roar is the only thing I can hear as I shout Zoe's name. She's on her stomach a few feet away, one of the columns of lockers lying across her legs.

No! I spring for her and toss the metal monstrosity aside. She flips over—thank fuck—but pain tightens small lines around her eyes. Her lips move, but my hearing has not returned to normal yet, and her words are unintelligible. Her actions, however, are not. She gestures behind me, and when I look over my shoulder, all of my anger and fear finds a target.

Through the dust, I make out two men stalking towards us from the far end of the structure. One has a large, tubular weapon positioned on his shoulder. The other carries what looks suspiciously like an AK-47. And behind them? No. No, no, no. Regina.

Grabbing Zoe's hand, I pull her up and start to run for the stairs, but a fiery projectile whistles past us—only a foot away from my head. I barely have time to wrap my arms around my partner, spin, and use my body as a shield before the ordinance hits. Something slams into my back to the right of my spine, knocking the breath from my lungs.

For a precious second, the world stands still, and then every fiber of my being is consumed by agony. Zoe writhes under me, yelling right in my ear. "Sin! Get up! We have to move!"

With a groan, I roll off her, and she pushes to her knees as she draws her weapon.

"Call for backup!"

"There is...no backup that can...get here in time. Regina..." The only thing saving us now? Our damaged hearing and roar of the burning cars all around us. Otherwise, the Fae would have already compelled us into obedience. Gritting my teeth against the pain, I search for a way out. A diversion. Somewhere we can survive another blast.

After firing another two shots at the men, she glances back at me. "Oh, God. Sin. There's...a piece of rebar sticking *out of your back!*"

"Do you think I had not noticed?" I snap. My strength is fading quickly. Too quickly. "Help me up. We must get closer to the stairs."

Zoe takes my arm and drapes it over her shoulders. We stumble towards the twisted metal and pile of rubble, ducking behind a mangled car. "We're sitting ducks here!" She fires another shot, then drops into a crouch.

"I can get us out," I manage, my voice cracking on every other word. "But only if I..." Fuck. I promised her I would not feed from her. But if I do not, we will both die. Or worse. I have no choice. Better to beg for forgiveness than to watch her descend into madness at Thorn's hand.

Zoe arches a brow. "Holy shit, asshole. Are you *asking* if you can feed from me when there's a guy with a fucking rocket launcher reloading a hundred feet away?"

Zoe shoves the pistol into its holster, then tangles her hands in my hair and slams her lips against mine.

Fuck me. She tastes like watermelon and fresh rain. The heady mix of her fear and arousal flows through me, and I cup the back of her neck, guiding her into my lap. I want her. All of her. From her soft moans, she feels thee same.

I could spend years kissing her. Decades. Lifetimes. But as soon as the telltale prickle starts along my shoulder blades, I pull hard on the tether between us, soaking up as much of her energy as I can in this final moment, then break off the kiss.

"You...will not like what comes next, my little pearl. Hold on."

A furrow deepens between Zoe's brows, despite the high that comes from such a deep feeding. "Sin?"

I stand in one fluid motion, ignoring the piece of rusted metal still embedded in my back, and strip off my jacket. Bullets pelt my chest, but they bounce off harmlessly—save for leaving burned holes in my shirt.

The corner of the garage glows from the power flowing through me, and with a roar, I break the chains I have kept locked since Lucifer released me from Hell. My wings burst forth with a great *whoosh*, I scoop Zoe into my arms, and take off at a run.

The man with the AK-47 continues to fire, despite Regina trying to shout in his ear, and I wrap my wings around my partner to shield her, picking up speed with each step.

A wave of celestial energy—a power I did not know I could still muster—sends both men and Regina flying back, and I slam into the concrete wall hard enough to burst through into a back alley where I let instinct take over.

Zoe screams as my feet leave the ground, locks her legs around my hips, and buries her face against my neck.

I doubt she will be able to hear me, but I have to try to reassure her. "You are safe with me, Zoe. I promise."

SEVENTEEN

Zoe

We're flying. Holy fucking shit, we're actually flying. My partner has *wings*. Beautiful black wings that make almost no sound as he carries us over the city.

His blood soaks into my sweater, and when I find the courage to open my eyes, his expression is pained and his skin pale. The steady beat of his wings falters, and we tumble maybe twenty feet before he regains control and turns, making a beeline for a tall building in Pacific Heights.

As we land on a narrow balcony, he loses his balance, and I do my best to keep him upright, but I feel like I've had half a bottle of Jack on an empty stomach—dizzy and weak and freaked the fuck out.

"Sin. Keep it together." I try to force some strength into my tone, and he blinks hard, then buries his face in the curve of my neck to stifle a groan. The sound startles me, as does the intimate contact, but only for the split second it takes me to realize his wings are now *gone*. "Where are we?" I ask when he tries to straighten, fails, and leans heavily on me once more.

"My place."

The balcony door is unlocked, thank God, and I try not to gape as I help him through the lavish living room and into the bathroom where he half-sits, half-collapses onto a plush, black rug over tile that probably cost more than I made last year.

"You have to remove the rebar," he grits out and flops onto his stomach. "I will heal…"

The last word is barely audible, and when I gently slap his cheek and call his name, there's no response. Shit.

Move, Zoe. You can do this. He needs you.

His black shirt is already shredded from the bullets and his wings, and I tear it from his body in long strips. They'll do until I find a first aid kit. "This is going to hurt," I say as I wad a length around the thick piece of metal protruding from his back and then wrap my fingers around the rebar. Bracing myself with my foot against his hip, I pull. Hard.

The sound. Oh, fuck. You don't ever forget a sound like that. But the metal clatters to the floor, and blood soaks the wadded up material. "If you were lying to me about healing, I'm going to kill you."

Smart, Zoe. You'd be killing a dead man.

Despite my fears, when I swap the soaked remnant of shirt for a thick black towel from the rack, the bleeding has slowed, and the edges of the wound look almost as if they're starting to knit back together.

Mostly convinced he's not going to die in the next few minutes, I crawl over to the sink and pull myself up. My eyes are sunken, almost bruised, and I'm covered in cement dust, dirt, and Sin's blood. My legs ache where the lockers fell on me, and my shoulder throbs.

My partner still hasn't moved, but he's breathing, so I

rummage around in drawers and cabinets until I find a fully stocked first aid kit and extra towels.

Everything is pristine—or was until he bled all over the floors—so I take off my boots before I rush through what has to be one of San Francisco's top ten most expensive places to live in search of the kitchen. I pass a *media room,* for fuck's sake.

But I come back with a bowl for warm water and more towels. "Sin?" His eyelids flutter, but that's the only indication he can hear me. "It's way too early in our partnership for this. I'd say you owe me, but you saved my life, so I guess we'll call it even."

Babbling steadily, which has to be my brain's way of keeping me from losing my shit, I strip off his pants, socks, and —sweet Jesus—his boxer briefs. The man has an ass I could bounce a quarter off of. Even with so many long-healed scars, he's magnificent, and I think I say that at one point when I swipe a washcloth over his hip.

I wish I could stop here and drag him to his bed, but the man is fastidious to a fault, so I have to roll him over and clean off the rest of the blood.

I slide my hands under his bulk—one at his hip and another at his chest, and I'm about to heave when he whispers, "Zoe. I can...manage once I can stand. Help me get to my knees first."

It takes us three tries, and my high school principal, Sister Margaret, would be horrified that I don't avert my eyes from the very impressive full frontal view of him I get as I help him to the shower and turn on the faucet.

With his hand braced against the marble, he grimaces, then steps under the spray with his back to me. "There is another bathroom down the hall with spare towels and a robe in the linen closet. You are running on pure adrenaline. Unless you want to sleep covered in my blood—which I would prefer you do not as my sheets are all thousand thread count, I suggest you clean up now."

I'm about to snap at him for not caring if I pass out when he glances over his shoulder at me, a glint in his eyes. "Though I would prefer you join me in here."

"I'll be fine on my own, thank you. And I'm not going to sleep here tonight."

I stalk out of the room, but I swear I hear him say, "We'll see about that," as I slam the door behind me.

Sin

She knows. As does Regina and the humans who attacked us. Only two in this realm had any idea of my true parentage before today: Maddox and his partner, Killian. Not even Commander Eve knew.

Now... I fully expect the commander to call at any moment. If she has not done so already. I have no idea where my phone is, or if it is still functional. Certainly someone noticed an angel flying over San Francisco.

The pain from my injuries was so great, I do not believe my glamour hid us well enough. Even so, Regina and her two human minions had plenty of time to see exactly what I am.

As the hot water runs down my aching back, I scour the fragmented memories from my time under Thorn's control. My one act of rebellion. I only managed to hide my angelic origins from him because I refused to accept them myself. But when I dragged him and Regina down to Hell, did he find out then? Or, perhaps, did Lucifer somehow let it slip?

Incubi are capable of flight, but a full-blood incubus has wings covered in skin, not the long black feathers I brazenly put on display. He may not have known before, but he certainly knows now. And that will only stoke his desire to capture me yet again.

When the water runs clear, I wrap myself in a towel and listen. There is no noise from the guest bathroom. No sounds at all. Fuck. If Zoe left, I will have to find her. She is in danger now because of me. Because she was seen with me.

Given how much I took from her, I am amazed she had enough left in her to care for me. And then the truth hits me. I left her alone. She could have passed out in the shower. Or worse...what if she opted for a bath?

Panic shoots through my limbs, giving me speed I should not have to race through the penthouse. I do not breathe until I find her curled on the floor in front of my closet with one of my shirts draped over her naked body.

"Zoe." On my knees, I cup her cheek and run my thumb down her neck. Her pulse is steady, if a bit slow, and she makes a small sound of displeasure as she tries to bat my hand away.

"Lemme sleep," she slurs.

"I will. But not here." I do not have long before I am forced to join her. And when I wake, I will again require sexual energy to complete my healing. Now that I have tasted her, felt her give to me willingly, I wonder how in the world I will ever be satisfied taking from another.

Scooping Zoe into my arms, I relish the warmth of her skin, her scent, and the way she nestles closer to me. But she did not ask for this. To be fed from so deeply, her own energy stores are almost gone. I hurt her, and it does not matter that she offered herself up to me.

It is not easy to maneuver her arms into my shirt without waking her, but after a few moments, I do up the buttons, and she is blessedly no longer bared to me. My dick is hard as steel, and I burn with need for her. I have never felt this way about anyone I have fed from. But my exhaustion grows heavier with each passing second until it overwhelms my arousal.

I barely manage to pull on a pair of boxer briefs before I collapse into bed next to her and draw the blankets over us. With my last shred of awareness, I withdraw my backup cell phone from the nightstand, power it on, and send the commander a message.

Attacked. Need cover story for explosions under James Temple's building. We are safe, but need rest. Will check in tomorrow.

Eve will find a way to explain the destruction of the garage. As for the angel soaring over San Francisco...no one will be able to explain that.

EIGHTEEN

Zoe

My body aches. Like I ran a marathon without training a lick. Every muscle seems determined to tell me how displeased it is, and stretching my legs feels damn near impossible.

It's dark, and my brain's fuzzy. This isn't my apartment. Or my bed. And...holy shit. I'm not alone.

I sit bolt upright, immediately regretting the motion as the room spins and I collapse back against the pillows with a grunt.

"Zoe." Sin's deep voice rumbles to my left, and I suck in a sharp breath. "Stay calm. You are in my bed."

"Your bed?" Knowing where I am is great and all, but Sin and I are *not* together. And the only way I'd ever sleep with him is if... "Oh, God. You used your *talents* on me."

I try to scramble away, but Sin bands his arm around my waist and pulls me back against him. He's so warm and solid, and the closeness calms something deep inside me, but it shouldn't. He...*fed* from me!

"You gave me permission, Zoe. We would have died. What is the last thing you remember?"

I can barely keep my eyes open. Is he still influencing me? My thoughts wander. Tacos. Orange blossoms. Pain. "We were at Temple's apartment. The garage." Large, black wings. Seeing the city from high above. Flying. Oh, my God. We were *flying!* "Oh, shit. You're...you have *wings!* How do you have wings?" I struggle to free myself from his hold, but he's too strong, and when his lips brush the shell of my ear, the intimate—and oddly familiar—gesture tamps down my panic enough so I can breathe.

"I am only part incubus. My father was an angel." His words are quiet and almost resigned, as if he doesn't want to recognize this part of himself. Or admit to it.

"Why didn't you tell me?" I roll over so we're facing one another, though it's pitch dark in here, and I can only just make out his profile as he stares at the ceiling.

His body stiffens, and he pulls the blankets over me with dispassionate precision. "I do not tell anyone. And you cannot either."

"Okay."

"Okay?" Shock roughens his tone, and he pushes up on an elbow with a groan. "That is your only response?"

Our brush with death is fresh in my memories again, and I shudder. "Sin, you saved our lives. You *flew* us out of that garage, past two men and a Fae who wanted to kill us—or turn us into zombies—and halfway across the city. With a piece of fucking rebar sticking out of your back. What do you expect me to say? Besides...'thank you'?"

Sin falls back down next to me. "You are truly unique in this world, Zoe. I am not certain any other, be they human or divine, would have been this...accepting. Or calm."

"I do have a question." It's getting harder to stay awake, and

I curl away from Sin and burrow deeper under the blankets, suddenly chilled. He follows, warming me with his body pressed to mine.

"Ask."

"You have this huge apartment. I'm pretty sure I saw a guest room. Why am I in your bed? I took a shower, but after that...everything's fuzzy."

He sighs, his breath warm against my cheek. "You gave me more of your energy than I thought possible." His voice too takes on a sleepy, slow cadence. "I was worried for you. Staying close will help us regain our strength faster."

"Is that—" I yawn, "—the whole answer?"

"No." Sin runs his nose along my neck with a satisfied hum. "I did not wish to be parted from you. I needed to hold you and ensure you were safe. Sleep now, Zoe. In the morning, things will return to normal."

He sounds so sad, as if "normal" is the last thing he wants. And as I drift off, I think it might be the last thing I want as well.

THE SCENT of coffee rouses me, and when I stretch under the expensive sheets, my body feels almost healed. Except for my legs. Reaching down, I find bruises along the backs of my thighs, just above my knees.

The lockers. They fell, pinning me, and Sin tossed them like they weighed nothing at all. A bathrobe lies across the foot of the bed, and I belt it tightly, my cheeks burning as I realize I'm naked other than one of Sin's silk shirts. At least it's long enough to cover...most of what needs covering.

My partner—clad only in a pair of dark pajama pants and nothing else—lounges on a cream-colored sofa in front of a gas fireplace, staring out the large windows at a view of half the city. Cradling the cup of coffee like it's the elixir of life itself, he doesn't move a single muscle unnecessarily as he takes a sip.

"I just brewed a fresh pot," he says, his gaze never leaving the skyline. "A courier will be here within the hour with clothing for you, but I am afraid I have little to no actual food here. If you tell me what you'd like, I will have it delivered."

I've just walked into an episode of *The Twilight Zone.*

"You had someone go buy me clothing?"

Slowly, he turns his head and focuses on me. The power in his blue eyes hits me square in the chest, and I take a step back.

"You would prefer to go into work wearing only my shirt? That can be arranged."

"I owe you an apology, then," I mutter as I pour myself a cup of coffee so strong, I'm actively wary of the first sip. "Clearly I took the 'right' side of the bed last night. You definitely got up on the 'wrong' one."

Sin cages me against the counter before I realize he's moved, and the mug slips from my hand. He catches it, but not before the hot liquid splashes my fingers.

"Fucking hell," he mutters and spins me towards the sink, wrenches the faucet, and thrusts my hand under cold water. "I do not know how to do this, Zoe."

"Do what? Avoid spilling coffee all over your partner? That's pretty damn simple. *Do. Not. Touch. Me.*"

"I cannot help it." His breath stutters, drawing my focus to his chest—and the heavily scarred but still damn sexy eight-pack ending in a *v* at his waistband. "I am drawn to you in a way I have never felt before."

"You're hungry," I whisper. "That's all this is."

"Perhaps. But I can control my appetites. What I feel for you is different." He shuts off the water and carefully dries my hand. "Does it still hurt?"

"No. Not...really." Hurt isn't the word. When Sin touches my fingers, little sparks of electricity run up and down my arm. He's not the only one who doesn't know what the hell is going on here. "Scale of one to ten. How hungry are you right now?"

"Six." Tipping my chin up, he meets my gaze. "You can tell by the color of my eyes. By how much red they contain. A ring around the blue means I have a day or more before I am compromised. When they turn completely red, that is when you must worry."

"They were red yesterday in the garage." He's still touching me. Still holding me, and dammit, I don't want him to stop.

Twirling a thick curl around one of his fingers, he inhales deeply. "And then you kissed me."

"You told me you could save our lives. I...had to. It was perfunctory."

"All you had to do was let me siphon off some of your energy. Instead of a simple kiss, you practically threw yourself at me. It was...far beyond perfunctory." Dipping his head, he brushes his lips to mine. "And most unforgettable."

"It can't ever happen again," I breathe, and whatever magic was flowing between us vanishes in a heartbeat.

A chime sounds, followed by a short knock. Sin releases me, turns on his heel, and strides down the hall. After a brief exchange of male voices, the door shuts again. "Your clothing," he says, dropping a bag on the floor at my feet before walking away.

And then I hear him start the shower. I'm so fucking turned on, I'm halfway down the hall before I stop myself. This has to be a side effect of letting him feed from me. I need to wash him off, figuratively and literally.

Each step causes Sin's shirt to rub against my over-sensitized nipples. Would he notice if I got myself off in the shower? If I don't, I'm not sure I'll be able to concentrate at all today, and there are still two demons out there hunting people. In the guest bedroom, I spread out the clothing he bought, then catch sight of the clock on the nightstand.

It's still early—not even 8:00 a.m.—and the distance between us, as short as it is, allows me to think. We were attacked around 5:00 last night and once we got back here, we never checked in with Commander Eve. Did anyone go to Loup Noir?

Rushing down the hall before I realize what I'm doing, I burst into Sin's bathroom. He's in the glass-walled shower, his dick in his hand, and his head thrown back as four separate jets spray his sculpted body. He's too far gone to notice me, and like some invisible force has tied a rope around my waist, I take step after step closer.

He's magnificent, and his moans of pleasure ratchet up my own arousal until he manages to form a word I can understand. "Zoe."

Me. He's fantasizing about me.

Like you aren't doing the same damn thing right now.

The voice in my head—the one that always gets me into trouble—won't shut up around him, and I wonder. Maybe if we gave in, just once, we'd get this out of our systems and could move on.

He says my name again as my robe falls to the floor, and from the size of the hard length in his hand and the speed of his thrusts, he's close.

Mine. The word rips through my very soul, and at this moment, the only thing I care about in this entire fucking world is getting my hands on him.

I don't bother stripping out of his shirt, just yank open the shower door and step inside.

Sin

I can almost feel her hands on me. Hear her voice tell me *she* wants to be the one to make me come.

Nothing and no one in my many centuries of life has ever made me feel like she does.

"Look at me, Sin."

I almost lose my balance when I open my eyes. She's here. Standing in front of me, soaking wet, with my shirt clinging to her slight curves. "What are you doing?" I can barely force the words out, but I need to know she wants this.

"Maybe...getting you out of my system. All I know is that I need you." Her fingers twist in my wet hair, and she tugs to the point of pain as she pulls me down for a kiss. I cannot help it when her arousal nourishes me, but this is so much more than feeding.

With her free hand, she strokes my shaft, her thumb sliding over the head, and the feel of her...it is too much. "Zoe.... Fuck!" I shout and lose control, jerking my hips and spilling my seed over her fingers.

The energy she gives off is intoxicating, and within seconds, I'm hard again. My desperate, overwhelming need partially slaked, I can take my time. Ravish her in all the ways she deserves, and all the ways I dreamed of as she slept in my arms.

"This must go." Buttons pop off the shirt, and the material shreds easily, leaving her exposed. So thin. So much pain and sorrow—more than one human lifetime should hold. And her scar. Even now, with her flushed pink from the hot water and her need, the raised skin almost glows.

There is magic inside her. An ability. And soon, we will explore it. But for now...

She weighs nothing and drapes her arms around my neck

when I lift her, hit the shower knob with my elbow, and carry her, both of us dripping wet, to my bed.

"Are you certain about this, Zoe? I need to hear you say it." I back away and avert my eyes. I will not take the chance that I am somehow influencing her without intent. She matters too much.

"Don't turn away," she whispers.

"I have to. Until you say the words. My gaze...I could unintentionally sway you."

Her hands smooth down my shoulders. "You walked away from me in the kitchen and I came to find you. I want this, Sin. I *need* this. I'm so aroused, and even when we first met, when I thought you were a total and complete asshole, I wanted you. I just refused to entertain the notion."

"We will still have to work together." The enormity of what we are about to do hits me. I am not strong enough to resist her. Not unless she puts a stop to this now. Zoe Dawes is everything I have ever wanted. Strong. Intelligent. Beautiful. And with no reservations about putting me in my place.

"I'm an adult. You're immortal. Pretty sure that makes you one too. Are we going to talk this to death? Or are you going to finally kiss me like you mean it?"

The husky sass to her voice pulls a growl from my throat, and I spin around, grab her wrists, and pin her to the mattress as I straddle her. "I do not *do* gentle."

"And I'm not made of glass." Her lips twitch in challenge, and that is all I need. She will be mine. If only for today.

NINETEEN

Zoe

His predatory gaze should scare me, but he crushes his lips to mine and suddenly all I want is to devour him. He tastes of coffee and strength and power, and unlike when he fed from me in the garage, I don't feel like I'm lost in him. It's the opposite.

I've found something. I take as much as he does, and my body tingles all over, power flowing through me. "You are delicious," he growls, trailing kisses along my jaw to my neck. Desperate to feel him—all of him—I dig my fingers into the hard muscles of his ass and pull him closer, trapping his length between us.

I want him inside of me, but more than anything else, I need to come, to have him play my body like a musical instrument—one where he controls all the strings.

Firm lips clamp around my nipple, pulling a moan from somewhere deep inside. More. Closer. Harder. "Sin. Please." My back bows as he bites down, and his fingers trail along my stomach, resting for a moment on the scar from Temple's bullet, and then dancing over my mound.

"Perfection," he says, meeting my gaze as he settles between my thighs. "I am going to make you scream, my sweet Zoe."

The first swipe of his tongue through my folds sends me shooting into the stratosphere, and if this isn't the most intense, amazing moment in all of time, I don't know what could top it.

With firm strokes, he urges me higher, then slides one finger into my slick channel. It's not enough. Not nearly enough. "More!" I pant.

"In time," he grunts around my clit. "I intend...to make...this last."

Teasing me over and over again, he brings me right to the edge of release, then crawls up to kiss my lips. I taste myself on his tongue, and I want to touch him, to wrap my fingers around his cock and make him as desperate as he's made me, but every time I try, he pins me down and tells me not to move.

I've never been one to take orders—not even in the bedroom—but with Sin, it's all I want to do. Well, that and take him deep in my mouth. Or have him press me up against the wall. Or...so many other variations.

We're both drenched with sweat when he fills me with three fingers, and I cry out at the sudden invasion, the perfect mix of pleasure and pain. My core clenches, starts to throb and pulse in time with his tongue, and as I scream his name, a great rustling sound fills the room, and the pressure of the bed against my back falls away.

Holy shit. We're...floating. Sin locks his gaze with mine, watching as I come undone, my body rocked by the aftershocks of the most intense release I've ever felt. "In this form," he says, his voice strained and rough, "I cannot carry disease. But—"

"I'm on birth control." Sweet Jesus I need him inside me,

and even though there's so much we don't yet know about one another, I'm certain of one thing. This man—demon—angel—doesn't lie.

With a roar, he plunges into me, his wings whipping the air around us into a storm. A chair overturns, the bedsheets tangle in the corner, and his cheeks redden, a vein in his forehead bulging as he thrusts harder and harder.

"Kiss me," he demands, and I oblige, wanting every single part of us to be connected when he finally lets go.

I shouldn't be ready again, but I am, and with one arm holding me against him, he slips his free hand between us to toy with my clit.

"Oh, God. Sin. More. More, more, more..." I beg against his lips.

Another flap of his wings, and I'm pressed against the wall several feet off the ground, my angel's hips pistoning hard and fast until he roars my name. Pure and overwhelming ecstasy consume me, and everything else fades away until there's only Sin.

———

Sin

With Zoe in my arms, her head resting on my chest, I bring us down to the bed and force my wings to retract. It hurts like a son of a bitch every time I release them, but the rush of power and adrenaline that follows is addicting. And part of the reason Gabriel rarely visits this realm.

We need more time. Days to spend exploring each other's bodies. But we must soon return to the investigation. And reality, and I fear I will never have her this way again. There is something so *right* about this, about us together. Something more than simply the sating of a longstanding need.

"Commander Eve messaged overnight," I say as I twirl an auburn curl around my finger. "Cameras at Loup Noir did not capture any sign of Regina last night."

Zoe's sweet relief perfumes the air, and I marvel at how easily I can read her emotions without the slightest use of my talents. "So, what do we do now?"

"We have an hour. Perhaps two, if you'd like another go..."

She snorts, a very indelicate sound for such a tiny human. "I meant with the case."

"Oh." My disappointment surprises me. "We should ask Eve for additional agents. Form a task force to watch the most popular clubs. When I first...*knew* him, Thorn did not have a pattern as he does now. He took women as he saw fit. As opportunities presented themselves. If he had grown tired of toying with his previous acquisitions or knew of a demon interested in a woman with certain characteristics, he would send Regina—or me—out to hunt..."

"Why the change, then? Granted, we don't know the exact dates all of the women were taken. But it seems pretty obvious it's about every three days." Snuggling closer, Zoe trails her fingers along the T-shaped scars covering my chest. I do not remember most of the floggings, but memories of coming back to awareness covered in blood and in so much pain, I could barely move fill my nightmares. I cover Zoe's hand with mine, and she seems to sense my discomfort and changes the subject. "So, um...how come you didn't tell me you were an angel?"

I close my eyes, relishing her closeness for at least another few minutes. "It is complicated."

Zoe straightens the sheet, drawing it over us before sinking back onto the pillow. "I don't really have...friends, Sin. Acquaintances, sure. But friends? People I trust?" She ticks off a finger at a time. "My grandmother, one of my college professors—though I can't even remember his name right now—and Temple. I want to trust you. But I don't know you. Yesterday, you kissed me and then sprouted huge black wings. And just now...? We had sex *in the air!* Why would you hide that?"

"Because I have to." I stare at the ceiling. The light fixture is crooked, knocked askew by my wings more than once as we fucked. "If Thorn and Regina had found out...before...my crimes would have been even more legion. More...depraved. They would have used my power to do..." I cannot finish the sentence. The very idea of an angel being forced to corrupt souls is too much. "Regina knows now, and she will tell Thorn. They will never stop hunting me. It would be better if I simply...disappeared."

A hint of fear creeps into her voice. "You'd leave? Really leave...*me?*" The final word is so quiet, I think I might have imagined it, but when I meet her gaze, her eyes glisten.

This—us—cannot be. Every moment she spends close to me is a moment she is in terrible danger. Why did I think we could ever be? The knowledge that I must hurt her rips my heart from my chest, but my only hope to keep her safe may be to drive her away. Or disappear.

"You do not need me," I say, forcing an edge to my tone. "You got me 'out of your system.'" If I do not end this now, she will be hurt. As will I. And that is a risk I can never take.

"I know what I said. But...you don't think I actually believed it. Do you? After what we just shared?" After a full minute, she sits up with the sheet clutched to her chest. "Shit. You did, didn't you? This was just...getting laid for you. I can't believe I was so stupid. That I let you in. That I trusted you." Her voice cracks, and she throws her legs over the side of the bed and pushes to her feet, wavering for a minute and giving me the perfect view of her ass until she finds my bathrobe and shrugs into it.

Tears glisten in her eyes, but she blinks hard to force them away. "I won't be able to think straight until I wash *you* off of me. By the time I'm done, I expect you to tell me exactly how much I owe you for the clothing. I'll reimburse you for it within the hour. And we're *never* talking about this again."

My bedroom door slams, and a piece of my heart breaks off and crumbles into dust. For centuries, I forced myself to be cold, detached, and unfeeling. It was the only way I could survive.

The very first time I saw Zoe, my resolve started to falter. And in the garage, when it was either show my true self or lose her forever, I knew.

Zoe Dawes ignited a fire deep inside me, and I do not think the flame will ever die out.

TWENTY

Zoe

I can't believe I fucked my partner. Marching down the hall to his guest bathroom, I strip off the robe and yank the shower handle all the way to scalding. I need to wash his scent off of me, but more than that, I need to punish myself for even *thinking* there might be something between us.

He's an incubus. A sex demon. I don't care if he's half angel, the other half of him is designed to seduce. To control.

Stupid, Zoe.

But I still need to work with him. The missing shifters—and the men we haven't been able to identify—are depending on me. On us. I can't let them down.

Hissing as the water hits my skin, I realize the bruises on my legs aren't my only injuries. My elbow is scraped raw, my right hip is four shades of purple, and now that the high from sex has worn off, I feel like I was hit by a truck.

The irony of using Sin's shampoo and soap don't escape me. I'm going to smell like him—at least a little—all day. I should go home, but it's already almost 9:00, and if Thorn follows the timeline he's used for the past eighteen months, another woman will go missing by tomorrow at the latest.

Questions race through my mind like Formula One cars, zooming around so quickly, I can't focus on any of them for more than a second. Where is he hiding the women? Who is he selling them to? And where?

I can't take the blistering spray a second longer, and once I've wrapped myself in a fluffy black towel, I peek into the hall. Sin's bedroom door is closed, and I can hear rattling and thudding, like he's moving furniture or something. Then again, his wings did some serious damage to the room when he was—*stop it, Zoe.*

My cheeks catch fire as a vision of his naked body flashes through my mind, but I shove it down deep and examine the clothes he had delivered.

Shit. Everything's in my size. And expensive. Even the black silk bra and panties. The jeans mold to my ass, and the leather boots? They look completely unassuming, but when I take a step, it's like I'm walking on air. There's no way I can afford to pay him back. Not right away. He must have spent twice my monthly salary on one outfit.

Unless I want to get myself home in his bathrobe—or my bloodstained clothes from yesterday—I don't have much choice but to accept the gift. And the bastard knew it.

My bag, which also bears a number of dark red stains, is at least mostly intact, and while my phone only has ten percent of its battery left, I slip out without saying a word to him and call a Lyft.

I'll be steadier once I get to the Bureau. I have to be. These women's lives depend on it.

NO ONE LOOKS at me twice when I walk in, even though I feel like there's this huge sign over my head flashing *I had sex with an angel last night.*

At the coffee pot, I barely nod at Kunchin when I fill my mug, then grab my spare phone charger and battery from my desk and make a beeline for the upstairs conference rooms. I need to talk to someone, and I absolutely do not want to be overheard.

"Hey, Zoe," Dion says when the call connects. "I mean, Agent Dawes."

"No, Zoe's fine. This isn't exactly...um...Bureau business."

She laughs, a deep, husky sound through my earbuds, and I can just imagine her throwing her head back and smiling as she says, "Well, okay, hon. What's up?"

"Do you know much about incubi? I have questions, and the handbook was a little light on the answers."

"You have a handbook?" After a beat, she huffs. "I'm not surprised. So many of us know little to nothing about those outside our kind. Pity, really. We all fight the same battles. Anyway, I know a little. What's that partner of yours done now?"

The temperature in the room feels like it rises twenty degrees, and I shed the brand new black blazer I almost didn't take from the bag of clothing Sin bought me. Until I checked the temperature outside and realized it was in the forties. "I need to know about their talents. How long their influence can last, what they can do to their victims..."

"Did he feed off of you?" Her voice sharpens, the hint of outrage both embarrassing and welcome. "Hon, that's sexual harassment right there. I don't care who he is, you *work* together."

"He had to."

"You're defending him?" she hisses, the very feline tone full of outrage. "Zoe—"

I rest my elbows on the table and drop my head into my hands. "Just let me explain. We were attacked yesterday, and he was hurt trying to protect me. Seriously hurt. And I had a choice. Let him feed from me or watch him die alongside me. He...he actually *asked* as he was lying there bleeding all over me."

"Huh. Incubi don't usually have that level of control. He's old then. Really old."

Picking through yesterday's memories, I say, "At least six hundred."

"Holy shit. Hon, he's obviously careful as fuck. Most incubi and succubi are killed by their victims' jealous lovers long before that."

I choke back a sip of coffee. Dammit. I should have taken the time to add some creamer to this swill. "So how long does their influence last? After they feed, I mean."

"You said he asked, right?"

"Yes."

"What color were his irises?"

"Dark red. Even the whites of his eyes turned red."

"He didn't influence you, Zoe. He couldn't have. Using his talent to alter or influence a person's thoughts? It requires energy. If his eyes were pure red, he was fucked. Like about to die fucked."

Suddenly realizing just how close we came to not making it out of that garage alive, I set the coffee down and force a few deep breaths to stop the room from spinning. "You're...sure?" I wheeze.

"Pretty damn sure. Also pretty damn worried. Where are you right now?" Dion's voice takes on a motherly tone, and I answer automatically.

"Work."

"The Bureau's off of Portrero, right? You have time to get coffee with me? Like now? I think the rest of this conversation needs to happen in person."

I shouldn't. Both because this case has a major countdown clock over our heads and because talking about my partner to a civilian feels...wrong. But I don't have any friends in the world of the *other*—except Kunchin—and I'm definitely not going to talk to a coworker about this shit. If I'm honest, I don't have any friends in the human world either. Not really.

"I can be at the Blue Bottle Coffee on Sansome in fifteen minutes."

Dion sighs, her relief bleeding through my earbuds. "The first cup's on me."

***

Sin

I can hardly see past my fear when I enter the Bureau. Zoe left my apartment alone—with only a terse text message explaining she was going to take a Lyft into work. Thank fuck for the Fiat Spider I keep in the garage in reserve. The Audi is still at James Temple's apartment. Or at least I hope it is.

Zoe is not at her desk either. Why did I not impress upon her the immense danger she is now in? Regina saw her. Saw me expose my wings to save her life. Zoe has the mortal realm's largest target on her back, and she is galavanting around *alone?* I can still detect a hint of her scent, so she has not been gone long.

Before I try to find her, I have the tech department transfer my mobile number to my backup phone. My primary cell ended up in six separate pieces after the explosion. Within seconds, the device vibrates, and two text messages flash across the screen.

Commander Eve: Where the hell are you?

Zoe: Running an errand. Be back at 11:00 a.m. Don't bother me unless there's a break in the case.

The order stings. No, it does more than that. It slashes a knife deep into a heart I thought far too damaged to feel anything.

I have to work at summoning my anger. Usually so close to the surface, it has faded since I met Zoe, and that is unacceptable. Anger keeps me focused, and I require as much of it as I can muster now. Phone in hand, I jab the screen hard enough, I fear it will crack.

Where are you? I am coming to pick you up.

"Sinclair! Get your ass in here!" the commander shouts, her tone not one to be dismissed. She stares daggers at me as I approach, shoving her keyboard back and waving her hand towards her visitor's chair.

"About damn time. Where's your partner? She came in, then ten minutes later, bolted like her ass was on fire," Eve says, a distinctive high-pitched edge to her voice. She's close to a shift. Something is bothering her. Something more than my AWOL partner and the attack on our lives.

"Zoe had a personal errand to attend to. Apparently. I am waiting to find out where so I can pick her up." Sinking into the chair, I narrow my eyes at Eve. "What is wrong?"

"Salem is threatening to fire me."

I lean forward, tension prickling along the back of my neck. "Why?"

"Three hundred and forty-two thousand dollars of this division's budget is unaccounted for. The dicks in Salem believe I had something to do with it." Her talons tap against the desk, and the frustrated sound she makes as she throws her head back shakes the glass walls. Any higher pitched, and she'd probably have shattered them.

I scan the bullpen, seeing heads turn, agents whispering to one another. Eve notices and slaps her hand down on the button to engage the privacy screens. "Just fucking great."

"Get one of the witches to cast a truth charm."

Grayson's eyes darken, and she shakes her head. "I won't ever be under a witch's spell again. Which means I have to do this the old fashioned way. Spending the next few weeks neck deep in budget reports."

Pushing to her feet, she turns her back to me and runs her hands through her blond hair. "But not until you tell me *exactly* what went down yesterday."

HALF AN HOUR LATER, I have still not heard from Zoe, and my ire and concern are rising with each passing minute. The commander is satisfied that neither Zoe nor I sustained serious injuries, and she had two of the mages conjure memories of a gas leak for the SFPD officers.

Back at my desk, I run a trace on Zoe's phone. Blue Bottle Coffee. At least she is in public and not out chasing down a lead on her own. It takes me only a few moments to convince one of the ghouls to check up on her.

"*Agent Sinclair,*" the ghoul whispers to my mind when it returns. "*Agent Dawes is having coffee with a panther shifter named Dion.*"

I take a small measure of relief from the report, and pull up James Temple's last will and testament. Fuck. The date at the top is the day before he shot Zoe. There is nothing out of the ordinary about the text. Standard legalese, his name, date of birth, address, and the like. A small list of possessions bequeathed mostly to Zoe, his savings to be distributed to a handful of charities.

Nothing appears out of place until I zoom out and view the two-page document as a single image. A faint watermark darkens the paper, and I have to rotate the pieces several times before the image coalesces into something that makes my blood run cold.

The edges are uneven. Perhaps a bit lopsided. But it looks very much like an orange blossom. Fuck.

Thorn and Regina are most certainly sending me a message. They know I am in San Francisco, and they are counting on my fear leading me to make a mistake. One that will land me in their clutches once again.

After I order the ghoul back to Blue Bottle to watch over Zoe, I turn my focus to the human missing persons databases and begin my search for men between the ages of twenty-one and forty. The assholes who nearly killed us yesterday were wearing masks, but as I flew past, I got a very good look at their eyes. I can find them. I have to.

Zoe

Blue Bottle Coffee's tall windows let in the late morning light, and when I step inside, Dion waves me over to a table in the corner. She's already ordered, and my mouth waters at the sight of the steaming French Press pot and two cups.

"Guatemalan single origin," she says with an easy smile. An animal print sweater hangs off of one shoulder, a black bodysuit underneath, and her skin glows, not a single fur visible.

"You're a mind-reader," I say, sinking down across from her.

"Nah. Us coffee snobs just gotta stick together." She winks, then depresses the plunger. "Okay. Spill it, hon. What happened with your handsome jerk of a partner?"

I can't tell her everything. Not by a longshot. But if I don't get some of this off my chest, I'm going to implode. "We had sex."

The French Press rattles on the table. "Holy shit. You...and an incubus? Was it hot? They're supposed to be—"

"Dion!" I check the tables on either side of us, hoping no one heard her say the word incubus. "I am *not* going to tell you that. Shit. We are totally failing the Bechdel test right now, you know."

"You needed *Other* dating advice, hon. So that's what you're getting. Next time, we can start a book club. I like me a strong military man with a kick-ass heroine." She leans forward, a sparkle in her amber eyes. "Dish, Zoe. I haven't gotten any in a year."

I don't know how to...dish. Though, when did I last have a female friend? College? I can't remember just hanging out and talking...ever. "Every time I'm close to him, I want to tear his clothes off. Or hold his hand. And that's just not...me. I'm the least clingy woman you've ever met. But after Sin fed from me, it was like I couldn't get enough of him. Even now, I still want him."

Staring up at the ceiling, I run my fingers through my unruly curls, pulling hard at the roots as I try not to scream in frustration. My nipples pebble under the silk bra, and I curl inward, suddenly self-conscious Dion might see how aroused I am.

"Do you know anything about *other* mating?" the panther asks.

"Mating? Like...what happens in all those paranormal romance novels? Aren't those full of shit?" I cup the mug tightly, needing the rich scent and warmth to ground me.

"'Course they are. But every lie starts with a kernel of truth." After a quick glance around us, Dion scoots a little closer. "When I find my mate, I'll know. I'll smell 'em. That's how it works for shifters. Witches...they feel this instant connection. Magic on magic. With incubi...it's complicated."

"Of course, I get the complicated one," I mutter.

Dion reaches for my hand. "Complicated ain't always bad, hon. From what I've heard, incubi...when they find the one for them? They'll die before they betray you. They'll die to protect you. And they'll give you the best sex you've ever had for the rest of your life." With a wink, she sits back. "He wants you too, right?"

My cheeks catch fire, and I stare into the bottom of the mug. "Yes. He said what he feels for me is...'different.' Not just hunger. Something more."

Dion pours herself another cup of coffee and grins at me. "Well, Zoe...then I have one question for you. What are you going to do about your partner falling in love with you?"

TWENTY-ONE

Sin

Despite my hatred of the swill brewed in the Bureau's break room, I have been staring at my computer screen for too long. After I pour myself a cup, I turn to find Velma—one of the new vamp agents—close enough I almost knock into her.

"Sinclair," she drawls, her wide, violet eyes framed with thick lashes that flutter as she smiles. "I was hoping to run into you today."

"This is not a good time. If you will excuse me—"

"No. I'm afraid I can't do that. I need your help." Velma leans a hip against the counter next to me and trails her hand down my arm. "I caught a case where a succubus was poisoned. And I could use a...demonstration."

Arching a brow, I retreat closer to the threshold, anger stirring in my gut. "A demonstration?"

Velma follows me, her hands pressed to my chest. "I want to understand how incubi and succubi feed. And reading about it isn't the same thing as experiencing it. Wouldn't you agree?"

"Hey. You want to step back, bitch? Or should I report you to Other Resources?" Zoe forces herself between me and Velma, and the feel of her ass brushing against me stirs my arousal until I register how much danger she's just put herself in.

With a hiss, Velma bares her fangs, and Zoe's eyes widen. Before I can move, the vampire has Zoe pinned against the refrigerator, one hand wrapped in her curls, the other around her throat.

"Get away from her. Right fucking now," I snarl and shove Velma across the room.

The vampire rolls to her feet, her eyes changing from violet to blood red, and stares at Zoe like she's a lamb waiting for the slaughter. "Who the hell do you think you are, *human?*"

I can scent Zoe's panic, but I stopped feeding on fear after my time with Thorn, and my instinct to protect, to hold Zoe close and ensure nothing ever happens to her flares white hot. Wrapping my arm around her waist, I glare at the vampire with as much power as I can summon.

"I do not give *demonstrations*, Velma. Everything a Bureau agent needs to know about the *talents* of incubi and succubi can be found in the handbook. You think because the commander is preoccupied, you can do whatever the fuck you want? Hardly." Keeping Zoe close, I edge closer to the telephone mounted on the wall, then dial security. "We have a situation in the break room. Agent Velma Mont Clare just attacked and threatened my partner. Bring the silver cuffs."

By now, the Yeti and two of the witches have flanked us, ready to lend aid. The vampire is a new transfer, and has rubbed almost everyone the wrong way in the past two weeks. This...will be the end of her.

"You will regret crossing me," Velma says, her fangs lending a slight hiss to her words.

I snarl at her. "And if you *ever* put your hands on my partner again, I will personally stake you through the heart with a silver dagger."

If I were alone, I would bait the vampire further, but I will not risk Zoe's safety. Nor the others standing with us. Velma swears and curses us as the Bureau's security team drags her away in cuffs.

"Where are they taking her?" Zoe asks softly.

"She will be detained in the underground holding cells for a day, perhaps two, until she is sentenced."

She sucks in a sharp breath and wriggles free from my hold, her slight body still trembling. "Sentenced?"

"For attempted murder. There are certain crimes that are not tolerated in our world, Zoe. A vampire exposing your neck, fangs bared, eyes blood red? She was seconds from biting you, and she would not have stopped until she had drained you dry." I should be more delicate. Considerate. Gentle. But our world is full of dangers she has yet to learn, and I must protect her at all costs.

Even if we can never be together—if she never accepts me— she will always be mine.

Zoe

My neck aches from the vampire's fingers around my throat, and my legs aren't all that steady, but I refuse to let Sin help me back to my desk. I force myself to walk ahead of him, then as he pulls out my chair, I meet his gaze. "What the hell were you doing back there anyway?"

His brows shoot up. "I was getting coffee."

"And letting a vampire feel you up."

He grunts something that might be "fuck," before taking a seat at his desk and glaring at me. "You made it quite clear this morning that there was nothing between us. Is there some reason you *care* who I let *'feel me up'*?"

Because I was wrong.

That's what I want to say. Instead, I brace my hands on the desk and force strength into my tone. "Because she's going to jail. And she almost killed me." I swallow hard and keep my stare locked on Sin's very blue, very stormy eyes. "Is it too much to ask that my partner act like a fucking professional?"

He leans halfway across the desk, close enough I can smell his cologne. Or maybe that's simply his natural scent.

"Watch yourself, Zoe. You have seen a part of me I do not show to anyone. But this face? This side of me?" His lips curl into a snarl, and his eyes churn with emotion. "I am a demon, and I have killed more than I have ever saved. Do not test me."

Oh, I want to test him. A lot. Until this cold, calculated demeanor of his cracks and the *real* Sinclair comes back. The one who held me all night last night. Who stopped a vampire from killing me.

Arousal warms my core, and Sin's nostrils flare. Shit. I have to change the subject. Or get the hell away from him somehow. "I'm still waiting for the bill for the clothes," I say as I shove my hands under the desk so Sin doesn't see them trembling. "I won't be in your debt."

A muscle in his jaw ticks for a full thirty seconds before he finds his words. "I have more money than I can spend in a thousand of your lifetimes, Zoe. Keep the damn clothes. And gather your things. I believe I tracked down one of the missing men. His name, at least. And we have an appointment to speak with his brother in twenty minutes."

I DON'T WANT to be in Sin's Fiat sitting less than a foot away from him, having his scent wrapped around me.

"So, who is this guy?" I ask.

"There's a new tablet in my satchel for you. All of his information is on it." He stares straight ahead, his voice flat and hard, and I roll my eyes. Fine. I'll play his game. At least the tablet isn't likely to try to kiss me. Or make me care about it. Not unless other worldly technology is somehow sentient.

"Gregory Locke, twenty-nine years old. Hasn't reported to his job at the Fisherman's Terminal for two weeks. Lives alone. No forced entry, no signs of a struggle." Scrolling through the police photos, I enlarge one or two, hoping to find something...*anything*...that points to Temple or Thorn, but the police report is accurate. Everything looks...normal.

I sneak a glance at Sin. "You're sure this guy is with Thorn?"

He stiffens. "Yes. My vision is better than a human's. They were masked when they attacked us, but the scar on his neck is distinctive."

Enlarging Gregory's photo, I focus on the mark below his jaw. "It almost looks like a brand. The letter K?"

"Yes. From a Los Angeles gang. Gregory grew up there." Sin accelerates up a hill, and I grab the door handle. I know his reflexes are sharp, but I've never been a good passenger. He sighs and slows the car to a more reasonable speed.

"You're infuriating," I mutter quietly.

"Because?"

His mocking tone grates on me, and I roll my eyes again. "You're an asshole. Grade A. One hundred percent. Until you purposely slow down because you know I don't like it when you drive so fast. I can't reconcile those two sides of you, and it's making me crazy."

"I am trying to protect you, Zoe." His fingers tighten on the steering wheel, and the veins in his neck bulge as he takes a slow, deliberate breath. "I cannot deny what I feel for you. Nor do I want to. There *is* something between us. But if we give in —if I give in—you will be hurt and I could not live with that."

I don't know what to say, but circumstances don't give me the chance because Sin stops the car and pulls effortlessly into a parking space in front of Gregory's apartment building. .

"We are here."

TWENTY-TWO

Sin

Gregory Locke's brother, Nathan, doesn't speak as he leads us to a pair of couches in his sparse living room. "Kinda surprised to get your call," he says once we're seated. "The detective in charge of Greg's case said they didn't have enough evidence to continue the investigation."

"We are not affiliated with the San Francisco Police Department. Consider us...*independent* investigators." I focus my gaze on Nathan's brown eyes, prepared to employ my talents if he pushes too far. Mem-Clear is a last resort only—one I rarely agree to use.

"I don't care if you're with the clown brigade if you can find my Greg." The strain in his voice and the rather significant bags under his eyes speak to the close relationship he shares—or shared—with Gregory. "They said he probably just ran off. Found a girl or lost himself to drugs again. But he wouldn't do that."

Zoe taps her tablet screen a few times, then arches a brow

as she focuses on Gregory's photo. "Your brother had several arrests for drug possession with intent to sell back in Los Angeles."

"Greg was clean. He'd been clean for three years." Nathan reaches into his pocket and pulls out a silver chip. "We both were. Went to meetings twice a month, together. The last one was a week before he disappeared."

Zoe's tone softens. "I'm sorry. We had to ask."

"Comes with the territory," Nathan says quietly, then angles his head to show off the tattoo on his neck. "We got wrapped up in a gang when we were kids. I was fifteen, Greg was just thirteen."

Nathan falls silent as he scrubs his hands up and down his thighs. "That's why I know my brother wouldn't just run off. We got out together. Moved up here together. He wouldn't have left me."

This man is telling the truth. I would bet my life on it. "We need you to tell us everywhere your brother might have gone the night he disappeared."

TWO HOURS LATER, over mulitas from Tacos El Primo, Zoe and I find a bit of a peace. Perhaps it is distance from this morning's events, or the food, or the shared desire to honor the anguish of Gregory's brother. She's somber, but every few minutes, looks over at me or out at the water. Something in her gaze stirs a distant memory. One stolen from me.

Another pair of eyes, the same emerald green. Another smart mouth. Another set of long, elegant fingers that fiddled with...something. Not a bracelet like Zoe wears. Metal. Fuck. Chains. Thorn's chains.

I can almost see her. Almost touch her. Almost hear her

screams as she died reaching for me. The world stops, the plastic fork in my hand suddenly transforming into the whip he forced me to use to hurt her. To hurt all of them. I am no longer with Zoe. I am a prisoner. Chained. Starved. Beaten.

"Do not fear, my love. I will come for you soon," I whisper as Thorn calls for me and curses my slow response.

A hand wraps around my throat, cutting off all my air, and Regina's voice consumes my entire world. "You will answer truthfully, demon. Or you will die."

"I will answer truthfully." It is all I can do. I am powerless against the Fae, even as my love's emerald eyes plead for me to fight.

Thorn forces me down to my knees. "You think you can deceive me?"

With everything in me, I try to resist, but Regina's compulsion is too strong. "Yes."

He laughs, the sound grating along my spine. "Then you will watch her die."

"Sin?" Zoe touches my arm, and the fork falls from my hand, tumbling down the stone steps in the breeze coming off the bay. She rushes after it while I am still frozen in place, tosses it in a nearby trash can, and then hands me hers. "Are you okay?" The blue of the sky and the scent of the water chase the memories from my grasp. But a faint vestige remains, and I know now. Why I am so drawn to Zoe.

Whatever she is? The part of her that is *other?* It may be unique in this world—*she* may be unique in this world—but another woman centuries ago carried the same power she has. If only I knew what it was.

"Merely lost in thought. Nothing to be concerned with," I say, hoping she will believe me.

For a moment, she considers my words, weighing their tone, their truth. Apparently convinced, she asks, "What's next?"

Relief makes my reply easier. "Old fashioned police work. We visit every spot Gregory may have been, and we talk to as many people as possible."

Her lips twitch into a half smile. "At least that's something I'm good at. And we'll be back in the *human* world for a while."

Turning to her, I reach across the plates and cover her hand with mine, hoping she will not pull away. When she twines our fingers, something inside me warms. Another familiar feeling I need more of. Much more. "We will be in your world, Zoe. But that does not mean the danger is any less. Thorn and Regina have practiced the art of deception for centuries. Millennia, even. As far as I am aware, they cannot change their physical appearances beyond hair color and clothing, but with their particular *talents*, they can hide in plain sight. Disappear in an instant. And get to anyone. So I must ask you to do something for me."

"What?" Her face is so open, so expressive. Concern, curiosity, and a hint of fear all playing over her features on a loop.

"Stay by my side. Do not go off alone. Not until this case is over. No more errands like this morning. And at night, you will stay with me. My apartment is heavily warded, and we will be safe there."

"Sin—" Her shoulders jerk back, and she tries to pull away, but I grip her fingers tightly.

"Please, Zoe. You can take the guest room. You do not have to talk to me, or even see me. But after what happened yesterday, we cannot take the chance. I was careless this morning when I let you leave. My anger got the best of me, and I put you at risk. What you found on James Temple's will? The watermark? Were you able to tell what it was?"

"No. It just looked like some strange curved lines."

"It was anything but. Once I rotated the images appropriately, it was clear. Thorn and Regina forced Temple to write a new will the day before he shot you." Zoe flinches, but I have to impress upon her the seriousness of the threat. "The watermark was of an orange blossom."

"An...orange...blossom..." Her hand goes limp in mine, and I can see the realization in her eyes.

"It was a message. They are coming for me, Zoe."

"You. Not me," she says.

"The easiest way to get to me?" I bring her hand to my lips and brush a kiss to her knuckles before releasing her. "Would be to go after you."

<hr>

Zoe

The sun is flirting with the horizon by the time we return to Bureau headquarters. I'm exhausted, and all I want to do is spend an hour or two with Sin in private so we can talk. Really talk. The short bursts of time we've spent in the car haven't been enough to have any sort of meaningful conversation.

"The easiest way to get to me would be to go after you."

When he said those words, I wanted to smack him. The man runs as hot and cold as the ancient pipes in my apartment. But when he's hot, he's positively smoking. Possessive, protective, and about as alpha as they come. Yet still one of the most respectful men I've ever met.

The bullpen is nearly deserted. Kunchin waves from his desk, and I nod towards the break room. I need to talk to someone other than my partner-slash-lover-slash-most-annoying-demon-on-the-planet. And I need coffee. Now.

I can feel Sin's eyes on me as I walk away from him, but

when I toss a glance over my shoulder, he quickly turns to look at his computer screen.

"You all right, Zoe?" Kunchin asks, then hands me the carton of sweet creamer. "Velma was a powder keg waiting to blow. Good riddance. And I haven't said that about any other agent in my five years here."

"I'm fine. Just a little sore." In truth, my neck aches like a motherfucker, but I managed to cover up the redness with some foundation and powder, and we've been so busy interviewing people today, I've mostly ignored it. "Is she...?"

"We don't tolerate that shit here," he says. "She's headed to the vamp prison on Alcatraz."

"There's a vampire prison on Alcatraz? No, wait. Of course there is." Shaking my head, I lean back against the counter with a sigh. "I'd ask you to pinch me, but your hands are twice the size of mine and you'd probably break my arm totally by accident."

His laugh sounds almost like a bark, but it's such a happy, joyful noise that I forget he's *a yeti* and join in. So gently I almost don't feel it, he bumps my shoulder with his fist. "I may be big, but I'm a gentleman."

"Can I ask you something?" We stand side-by-side, staring out at the bullpen, and I can't look at Kunchin or Sin at this point, so I pin my gaze to the assignment board on the far wall. I'm not sure how I missed it before, but the San Francisco office of the Bureau only has a dozen agents. The rest of the people working here are all support staff. Crime scene investigators, Mem-Wipe technicians, researchers.

"Anything. I'm an open book." Kunchin turns and fills our mugs, then adds a truly unhealthy amount of creamer to both of them.

"You're like seven feet tall and covered with white fur. You don't...*live here*, do you?"

"Here? At the Bureau?" His ice blue eyes widen, but then he chuckles and pulls a small black box from his pocket. With the press of a button, the yeti's entire body seems to blink and vibrate for a split second, but nothing else happens. "Perception filter," he says. "Works on all humans."

"Um, I think it's broken."

Kunchin cocks his head, then shakes the box. "Dammit. If this thing's on the fritz again..."

My stomach clenches, and I brace my hands on the counter. "You said it works on all humans. But what about *others*? Does it work on them too?"

"Nope. It's coded for human eyesight only. Well, and human recording devices. This is the age of the cell phone video after all." He peers down at the box and fiddles with the buttons as I pull out my phone and snap a photo of him.

"Oh, shit." I show him the picture. In it, a tall, very well-built man with pale skin and snow white hair stares at the box in his hand. His very human hand. "It's working just fine."

I can't breathe, and my heartbeat roars in my ears. I need to sit down. No. I need— "Sin!"

He's at my side faster than I think should be possible, and he and Kunchin each take one of my arms to help me to my desk. "Zoe, what is it?" Sin asks.

"I'm not human..."

TWENTY-THREE

Zoe

"Talk to me, Zoe," Sin says as he takes my hands in his and searches my face. "What is wrong?"

"His...his per-perception f-filter. It d-doesn't work on m-me." The words don't want to come. Or maybe I don't want to believe them. "I'm n-not...not..."

Kunchin rests his hand—paw?—on my shoulder, then shows Sin the black box. "Bureau-issued perception generator. Hides this," he gestures to himself, "from human eyes."

"I know what it is," Sin snaps. "The shifters and the Fae carry them as well. What does this have to do with why Zoe is so upset?"

"It didn't work on her."

"And you are certain it is not broken?"

I hand Sin my phone with Kunchin's picture on it, and he glances up at the yeti. Swiping to the camera app, he takes a second photo, then frowns. "Leave us, please."

"Zoe?" Kunchin crouches down so we're eye-level. "That okay with you?"

Sin growls, but I shoot him a look that could kill—if he weren't immortal—and then return my attention to Kunchin. "It's fine. Just...don't tell anyone else, okay?"

Making the universal gesture for locking his lips and throwing away the key, the yeti lumbers back to the break room for his coffee.

"What am I?" I whisper. "Nothing makes sense anymore, Sin. My life... Who—or what—I am." Yet again, the sensation of being trapped inside my own body consumes me. I can't breathe. I'm frozen. But I can see Sin, his face drawn in worry, and then I'm back with him, in the Bureau's bullpen, and I stifle a sob.

"I would much rather discuss this somewhere I know we will be safe. Will you come home with me?" Sin asks.

"In a little over twenty-four hours, another woman is going to be taken. We have to figure out which clubs to stake out, keep working on the victim profile, try to find the other two men Thorn has..." If we keep busy maybe I can ignore what just happened for another few days. Maybe I can keep pretending I'm human until this case is solved and then I can fall apart. Because that's all I want to do. Fall apart and reexamine my entire life to see if I should have known.

Sin stands, pulling me up with him. "We can continue to work. I have plenty of equipment for both of us and an encrypted connection to the Bureau's databases. Trust me, Zoe. I want to solve this case more than you could ever understand. But there is one thing I want even more."

I tip my head back, meeting his deep blue eyes. The emotion in them makes me want to step away—or throw myself at him. Both options seem equally appealing. "What?"

"You. I want to help you understand what you are—who

you are—so that perhaps one day, you will accept what I feel for you."

Sin

Zoe has not said a word since we left the Bureau. At least she had already agreed to stay with me, and we'd stopped at her apartment after lunch for her to pack a few of her things.

As soon as we arrive at my home, however, she excuses herself to the guest room, and moments later, I hear a single sob before there is only silence.

Fuck. Human emotions are not one of my strengths. To give myself time to think, I call the building's concierge and instruct him to have a pizza delivered within the hour, then open a bottle of red wine, pour two glasses, and set them in the living room where we can look out over the whole city. I need to be able to see the sky.

"Zoe?" I call. "I am having food delivered. Will you join me so we can talk about what happened earlier?"

She stands in the door, stock still, a tear glistening on her cheek. Even upset, exhausted, with bruises darkening on her neck from Velma's attack, and bags under her eyes, she is beautiful. "Do you have any answers?"

"I have...theories. Some of which you may not want to hear." I offer my hand, prepared to scoop her up in my arms and hold her until she hears me out, but, resigned, she places her delicate fingers in mine and lets me lead her into the living room.

"You really do have more money than you could ever spend, don't you?" Zoe muses as she curls up in one corner of the couch and stares out over the city.

"An advantage of being as old as I am. Investing in a few key technology companies at their inception has proven very lucrative. I also own a successful human nightclub in the Mission District. Prior to meeting you, I would often find a willing *donor* there when I needed a meal."

"Prior?" Her voice holds a hint of uncertainty that I very much dislike. As if I could ever feed from another again.

Picking up the wine that probably cost more than two months' Bureau salary, I take a healthy sip. She is not ready to hear my declaration of...what? Love? Lust? Devotion? Even I am not certain. I do not think she is ready to hear any of what I have to say, but now that my memories are starting to return, I cannot keep this secret any longer. "You are a mystery to me, Zoe. I have been around *others* all my life, and you...make no sense. There is something so very familiar about you, yet until this morning, I could not put my finger on it. You are an unknown."

"Great. I'm cafeteria mystery meat." She gulps down half the wine before her eyes widen and her cheeks flush. "Shit. This is expensive."

After a wave of my hand, I drain my glass. "I have more. If you want to get drunk, it might as well be on something of quality."

Satisfied, she drinks it down, and I pour us both a second.

Shame is a powerful emotion, but I push it aside for her. "When I first saw you at the crime scene, I was quite rude to you."

"Understatement of the year," she mutters.

"Perhaps. But I had my reasons. I did not understand what they were at the time. I do now."

For too long, I stay silent, until Zoe nudges my shoulder. "I'm waiting, Sin."

"I had so few memories of my time as Thorn's prisoner," I

say softly. "I did not even know how I managed to break free and take him and Regina to Hell. Not until today." There are only inches between us, and I reach out to brush a knuckle along her cheekbone. "One of Thorn's last victims looked very much like you. The same eyes. The same spark of curiosity. The same biting wit."

"I don't understand," Zoe says. "Are you saying someone in my family—*six hundred years ago*—was Thorn's victim?"

"I do not know. She may simply have the same *other-ness* that you carry. Her name...she was called Genevieve. I did not help Regina capture her. You see, Genevieve was hunting Thorn on her own. She intended to be taken, to let herself be tortured and brutalized so she could find a way to end him."

"But none of the women ever escaped," Zoe says, shaking her head. "Why did this Genevieve think she could do it?"

"She believed she was immune to Thorn's mind control. Regina captured her, but the others who fell victim to the Fae's spell would remain almost catatonic for hours. Sometimes even a day after Thorn caged them. This gave him ample time to invade their thoughts, to discover their greatest fears. Genevieve recovered only minutes after being locked in her cage. I was on guard duty, and she offered herself to me."

Zoe's horrified expression grips my heart in a vise, and I rush to continue. "Not for sex. She offered to feed me so I would have the strength to help her."

Relief smoothes the lines around her eyes and lips. "And... did you?"

"It took much convincing. Too much. But yes. I fed off her energy—freely given—and I started to fight back. I wanted to free Genevieve that moment, but she refused my aid. 'There is only one way out for me,' she said. 'I must end him once and for all.'"

The doorbell chimes, and I curse under my breath. Zoe

needs food, but I do not want to be disturbed. Not now. With every word of my tale, I fear I will lose my resolve. With every interruption, that I will not have the strength to continue. "Stay hidden," I say sharply. "I would prefer no one—not even those I trust most—know you are here."

She nods, and a few minutes later, I return with the box of pizza and another bottle of wine.

"I'm not hungry," Zoe says, but I place two slices in front of her anyway before I take a seat, closer to her this time. I need her like I need my next breath, and I do not know how to tell her.

"You must keep up your strength. Eat *something* at least."

"Keep talking." She picks at a slice of pepperoni, pinning me with her unwavering emerald stare. "Or I eat nothing."

Genevieve's heart-shaped face, obscured for so many centuries, is now a permanent fixture in my mind. So similar to Zoe, yet the woman in front of me has a depth, an energy, and a spirit all her own. "Genevieve convinced me to help her. To give her as much information as I could about Thorn. About how he broke the others."

With a shudder, Zoe sets down the plate, and I arch a brow but continue anyway. "For two days, Genevieve endured Thorn's torture, and when I tended to her, to heal her enough for him to start anew the next day, she asked me question after question. She brought me back, Zoe. From a place where every second was endless agony, darkness, and despair. And yet, I could not do the same for her."

"What happened to her?" Scooting closer to me, so close our thighs press together, Zoe links our fingers, and her touch gives me the strength to continue.

"Thorn kept the women separated most of the time. He thought it would amplify their fear. They could hear one another's screams, but were only rarely in the same room. He occupied a network of tunnels that once served as a water system for Florence. The cisterns were perhaps ten meters apart. We... were not careful. I spoke too loudly, and Thorn—or Regina—I do not know which—heard us."

"Oh, shit."

"An appropriate response." Leaning my head against the back of the sofa, I stare up at the ornately carved ceiling rails and the light fixture I restored to its original beauty when I bought this building. "Thorn knew Genevieve had a form of magic within her, but he did not know what it was. She told me she had been blessed with a gift. One that would allow her to bind her consciousness to his and destroy him."

"And could she?"

I shake my head. "We never had the chance to find out. Thorn killed her in front of me. I was powerless to stop him, and after I cradled her dead body in my arms, he forced me to massacre all of the other women, then the men. He planned to start anew in another place. And he had chosen *me* to accompany him."

"He was going to keep you?"

"I was too powerful a tool to waste," I say quietly. "But Genevieve...the memory of cradling her in my arms as she took her last breath...it woke me up, if you will." I scrub a hand over my face. "I only wish it had not taken me so long to build up enough strength to fight him. If I had been faster, some of his victims might have survived. But in the end...I broke free.

"Thorn had never seen the part of me I keep hidden. My wings. My angelic talents. He did not know I had the power to visit Hell. All angels do," I add when Zoe's eyes widen. "I used my talents against him and Regina, stunned them so they could not fight back, and delivered them to Lucifer himself."

Zoe reaches over and brushes a tear from the corner of my eye. "I'm so sorry."

I press her fingers to my lips, then my cheek. "There is nothing that can change the past, my sweet Zoe. Only the future. You can help ensure Thorn's reign of terror ends here. I believe you may be descended from Genevieve's line. If so, it is possible you can resist his control as she did."

"That still doesn't answer the most important question, Sin." Zoe hasn't moved her hand away, and she leans closer so she can rest her head on my shoulder. "What am I?"

TWENTY-FOUR

Zoe

I feel almost normal nestled against Sin, the spicy aroma of pepperoni pizza mixing with the expensive wine and his own unique scent. He presses a kiss to the top of my head. "I do not know, my pearl."

"Pearl?" The idea that he's given me a nickname—one that obviously means something to him—is enough to make me chuckle. Or at least smile.

"An expression I picked up long ago. A pearl starts from a grain of sand inside its oyster."

"So, I'm an irritant. Something hard and foreign?" I should be angry, but the way he says the word…I like it.

"You are an unknown. A surprise. A beautiful, beguiling puzzle. And I very much want to figure you out." Sin leans forward, keeping me close, and retrieves our wine glasses. "Will you indulge me?"

"In what? A drinking game?" After today, I wouldn't say no

to a couple of rounds of shots, but not even someone as rich as Sin would play a drinking game with wine this good.

Sin chuckles. "No. Merely some questions about your past. And a test or two of your abilities." He takes a sip of wine, then stares into his glass. "You mentioned your grandmother when we first met. Can you tell me about your parents?"

"They..." I swallow hard. "I never knew them. They were in the army and they both died when I was eight. I don't even remember them."

"And your grandmother raised you?" Sin plays with my hair, then starts to massage my scalp in the most delicious way. Sexy, but also comforting.

"Uh-huh." The wine must be going to my head, because it's like I'm dreaming and awake at the same time. I'm here, sitting on Sin's couch, staring out over the San Francisco skyline, but I'm also somewhere else, somewhere I can't move, with a movie of my life playing out before me. "She always said I was her miracle."

"Why?" He brushes his lips to my ear, and I wish I could lose myself in him again. Like this morning—was it only this morning?—and forget about everything else. Thorn and Regina. Velma. Temple. All of it. "Zoe?"

"She was all alone," I say, the words hard to form now that he's moved on to massaging my shoulders. The wine gone, the pizza mostly untouched, it's just the two of us. Close enough it feels like we're one soul. "Said I came to her—oh, yes, right there—when she was about to give up. 'Like a gift from God,' she said."

"Do you have any photos of her?" Sin asks.

"On my phone." Snuggling closer to him, I reach into my pocket, enter my passcode, and scroll through the couple of dozen pictures I've taken over the past year or so. Shit. I need to get out more. These are the only ones I have? I'm pretty sure Temple's nieces take more photos in one day than I've taken since I got this phone. "Here. This is her."

After he eases the device from my hand, he stares at the older woman's smiling face. She's outside in a garden. Our garden from the little house in Novato with the apricot trees that bloomed every spring. I can feel Sin's frown as he studies Nana's photo. "Are you certain you were...related?"

I jerk up to find him tapping the screen, emailing himself the picture. "Hey. That's a shitty thing to say. Give me back my phone."

"Zoe, answer the question. It could be important."

"Nana was my father's mother. I can't..." Tears spring to my eyes and I blink hard to force them away. "She didn't keep any pictures of him. I don't remember him."

"Look at me, Zoe." Sin sets my phone down and cups my cheeks. "Listen to my voice and focus on me." His sapphire eyes darken, turning almost black, and my head starts to ache like a storm's coming in. "Tell me you love me."

"What?" Shoving at his chest, I push him back hard enough he almost tumbles over the arm of the sofa, then get to my feet. "This was a mistake. Coming here. Shit. You just tried to *use your talents* on me. To make me say something you *know* I don't feel. How could you?"

He rolls to standing and moves so quickly, he's between me and the door before I even register the motion. "I had to prove to you that you are *other*. I am very strong, Zoe. Perhaps one of the strongest incubi alive. My angelic parentage only enhances my power. And yet you, who believed you were human three hours ago, not only resisted me, but knew exactly what I was doing."

I can't do this. I can't...stand here listening to him with all of his logical excuses and rational explanations when my heart is beating half out of my chest. "Sin. I can't do this. Not tonight. Maybe not ever. I don't *want* to know what I am. I'm Zoe Dawes. Granddaughter of Seraphina Dawes. Human. Cop. And scared as fuck."

He calls my name as I race down the hall towards the guest room, and when I slam the door in his face, I know the anguish on his handsome features will haunt my dreams.

———

Sin

Seraphina. Her grandmother's name is *Seraphina?* As in the Seraphim. Celestial beings tasked with doing the Almighty's work. The most trusted. The most holy. And based on how she resisted me, Zoe's grandmother was *one of them?*

I pull out my tablet and examine the photo I took from her phone. Even the Almighty makes mistakes on occasion, and this is one of those times. Despite the photo's time stamp being a solid fifteen years ago, the digital metadata—the underlying code that marks where and when the picture was taken—is mostly missing. And what is there...*fuck.*

Two years ago. It was taken less than two years ago. When Thorn and Regina were mistakenly freed from Hell.

Zoe—my Zoe—is a celestial being. Of what sort, I have no idea. Why does she not remember? Why give her a human history, human memories, a very human personality, and send her here?

Tablet in hand, I stride for the guest room door, but just before I knock, I hear her crying. Everything inside me aches to comfort her, but her emotions hit me like a tidal wave. She is terrified of me. Of the moment we just shared. Of falling prey to my talents and losing herself.

Pressing my hand to the door, desperate for even a single moment of connection, I whisper, "You have nothing to fear from me. I will walk away before I will ever harm you, even though it will be the hardest thing I will ever do."

And it is. Each step towards my bedroom feels like I am mired in quicksand, and the pain in my heart deepens with every footfall. But eventually, I close the door. Tomorrow, we will need to find a way to work together to stop Thorn once and for all. But for tonight, I will leave her be.

***

Zoe

I've cried so much, my eyelids are swollen to twice their normal size, and I don't know how I'll ever sleep tonight. My head still aches from resisting Sin's influence—not that I even knew I was doing it at the time—and as I flop down on the bed, all I see are images I don't understand.

Dark stone. Blood. Flames. And Sin. But not like he is now. Could...could he have left me with some of his memories when he fed from me? That's not possible. Is it?

It's still early, and while I"m exhausted, I'm not sleepy. So I pop in an earbud. I need a friend. Need to take my mind off of everything that's happened in the past forty-eight hours. But as I dial, it strikes me as so odd that I literally only have one person I can call.

"Hey, hon," Dion says, her voice smooth. There's music in the background, but it's quiet, relaxing. Jazz or maybe Blues?

"Hi. Um, shit. I didn't even think. You're not working tonight?"

"Nope. I'm only at the club on weekends. I work the streets the rest of the time." As soon as I start to sputter because I'd never have guessed she was a sex worker, Dion chuckles. "Oh, I wish I could see your face right now, luv. I'm kidding. Kinda. I'm a counselor for at-risk BIPOC and LGBTQIA+ youth in the *other* community. Which usually involves me walking the streets of the Tenderloin and the Haight all day."

"Maybe I've been on the job too long," I say. "Before I joined the Bureau, I was with the SFPD. You had me worried all my supposedly 'finely-honed' investigative instincts had failed me. Which...after the day I've had... I'm starting to worry I shouldn't be in this line of work."

"Zoe, every single thing about you screams cop." The music in the background quiets. "What happened when you went back to the office? If that demon was an ass to you—?"

"No. He actually wasn't." With a sigh, I curl my legs up and settle back against the pillows. "This is about me. I'm not... fuck. Dion, there's something about me that isn't human."

I'VE CATALOGED every single line and whorl of the ornate cornices in Sin's guest room, and I still can't sleep. Talking to Dion helped, but it also highlighted just how "different" I am. She has all these amazing, vivid memories of her parents and sister, her first shift, even her high school prom. And me? I can barely remember my mother's voice. Or getting my driver's license. All those big life events that should have made an impact on me? That should have shaped who I am? They're like faded photographs I can only see from a great distance, and that terrifies me.

My stomach growls, reminding me that I haven't eaten since lunch. Sin's been quiet for a few hours, and it's late enough he's probably asleep, so I pull on a robe I find in the closet and pad out to the kitchen for a piece of cold pizza.

The city sprawls out before me, bright lights, cars zipping through the streets, a few people far below dotting the sidewalks. And the water. San Francisco Bay stole my heart the first time I saw it. I know that as well as I know my own name, but...the memory of that day is fuzzy too. I know my grandmother was there, her hand on my shoulder. It was sunny. The wind whipped my curls into my eyes, stinging my cheeks.

"This is your home now, Zoe," my grandmother had said. "Until the end. I will not always be here with you, but you are never alone."

Tears burn the corners of my eyes. The easy friendship I've found with Dion? At the moment, it's all that's keeping me sane. Because the only other people in my life I trusted—my grandmother and Temple—they're gone. Nana lied. I *am* alone.

Trudging back towards the guest room, I stop when I hear a low moan from the master suite. Then a loud thud. "Stop... please," Sin slurs, and I don't pause for a second before rushing into his room.

Oh, shit. He's naked, huddled on the floor with his wings folded against his back. His eyes are closed, and I don't think he's awake, but he rocks back and forth on the balls of his feet, reaching out for something he can't seem to grasp.

"Do not...take her..."

Her. His Genevieve. An intense burst of jealousy prickles over my skin, but it vanishes as soon as he cries out again. "No!"

The anguish in his voice...it breaks my heart, and I drop to my knees to wrap my arms around him. "Sin. Wake up. It's Zoe. Come back to me now. Please."

His embrace threatens to crush my ribs, and I can't breathe. "Sin," I croak. "Sin!"

"Fuck." He draws the word out, like he's pouring all of his

pain into the single sound, and shifts me closer, still holding just as tightly, but in such a way I'm no longer worried about passing out. "Zoe. Do not leave. Not again. Never again."

"You're not making any sense—"

"I will not survive losing you again." He buries his face in my neck, inhaling deeply. "I understand now."

"I don't. Sin? What's going on?" Wriggling back far enough I can meet his gaze, I beg him for answers, but he shakes his head like he's just now realizing I'm here in his arms, despite saying my name.

"Stay with me," he whispers, lifts me, and gently deposits me on the bed. "I need you close."

I don't have the heart—or the strength—to tell him I'm not going to have sex with him again. But when I try to scoot to the edge of the bed, he stops me, cupping my cheeks and kissing me. It's not a demanding kiss. It's a desperate one. Like he's terrified I truly am going to disappear if he lets me go.

"Don't try to glamour me," I say against his lips. "It's not right."

"I will not. I cannot." Warm fingers cup the back of my neck, and his eyes...they're wild, but his irises are bright blue, honesty shining all the way down to his soul. "You are immune to my charms, Zoe Dawes. But I am afraid I have lost myself to yours."

"I have no charms. Whatever I am, Sin...whatever powers I might have? I don't know how to use them. I don't think I ever will."

"You are wrong, my sweet pearl. You will find them when you need them most. That is how it has always been. And when you do, I am afraid we will never have this," he gestures between us, "again. Give me this night? Let me worship you like I have dreamed of. Let me show you how much I lo—how much I care for you."

He turns his head, trying to prove to me he isn't influencing me at all, and all I want is to see his eyes again. To feel his lips on mine. To be one.

I slide my fingers into his hair and gently turn his head so our gazes collide. "Show me, Sin. Show me everything."

TWENTY-FIVE

Sin

I must be dreaming. Zoe is curled against me, her hair tickling my nose. The scents of our coupling mix with watermelon and coconut, and I do not ever wish to move from this spot. She does not know yet. Who she is. Who she was. Who she will be once again.

But I do. And when the pieces all fell into place, I could not breathe from the weight of it all. I know what is coming for her. What she will try to do and what it will cost her. I will find a way to save her. I have to. What I do not know is whether she will forgive me. Or how much time we have until the end.

"Zoe. My love, wake up." I cringe as I let my feelings for her slip through the wall surrounding my heart. As we came together for the third time in the early hours of the morning, I knew I could deny it no longer. I love her, and I always will.

If only Fate were not so cruel, conspiring to keep us apart. Even now, with Zoe naked in my bed, her lips swollen, her eyes sleepy, I can feel the distance between us growing. Once she accepts the truth of who she is, she will leave me. She will have no choice.

"Hmm?" She is still in that blissful state between asleep and awake where anything seems possible. Where one can choose to stay in their dreams just a bit longer or return to the real world.

Kissing her gently, I try to ease us both back into the world of dreams, but our phones ding simultaneously. Hers from the guest room, mine on the bedside table.

"Stay here," I urge as I wrap my arm around her waist. "It's the commander. We are being summoned."

"Shouldn't we go then?" Despite her words, she settles against me with a sigh, and I pick up my phone so we can both see the screen.

Another body turned up this morning. Corner of Castro and Pine. Get down there. Now.

"Shit," Zoe says and sits up. "We're out of time, Sin. He's going to take another woman tonight."

"I know." Throwing the phone down on the bed, I hold her close. I need one more moment with her. One more embrace. One more kiss. "Promise me something, Zoe."

She tips her gaze to mine, uncertainty and so much more churning in her green eyes. Concern. confusion. Maybe even... love. "What?"

"You will be careful today. Stay by my side. Do not take unnecessary risks." Capturing her lower lip between my teeth, I bite down just hard enough for her to feel it for the rest of the day. Everything I am belongs to her. It always will.

"I'm a cop," she says when she pulls back, her cheeks flushed. "I still am, even though I carry a different badge. My job is to take risks to protect the innocent. If I don't, they die, and I can't—"

"This is different," I say sharply. "This is Thorn. Even a single risk could get you killed."

"You're not my keeper, Sin. You're my..." She stares down at our linked fingers, then lets her gaze rove over my chest. "You're my partner. But you're also more. Something...we haven't figured out yet."

Say it. Please. Do not get out of this bed without remembering who you are.

"I'll be careful." She brushes her lips over a long scar just below my collarbone. "Because I want to figure it out. Figure *us* out."

It is not enough, but at the same time, more than I could have hoped for. More than I had centuries ago. More than I may ever have again.

Zoe slides from my embrace and runs a hand through her mussed curls. "I need a shower." Her lips curve into a smile. "I don't suppose you'd like to join me?"

Before she can take another step, I scoop her up and cradle her to my chest. "I would like nothing more."

Zoe

Every step is pure torture with Sin next to me. It's like my body is completely attuned to his presence, and my swollen lower lips rub against my clit as we walk up Castro to the crime scene.

Focus, Zoe. Someone is dead, and you're thinking about banging your demon partner again. Ridiculous. You're a fucking cop. Act like it.

He took me twice in the shower, then made me coffee while I dressed and tried to calm myself down. On the way here, he stopped so I could get a breakfast sandwich, and now, he stays close but doesn't touch me. I think he's afraid if he does, we'll be all over one another again and won't be able to stop.

There's something more in his blue eyes this morning, though.

Fear.

We don't need to show our badges to the crime scene crew. They recognize us, and what I now know are magical wards that hide the street from view admit us into a private, gruesome cocoon.

The young woman's body isn't arranged as reverently as Jacinda's. No. She was dumped. Quickly and without ceremony. Her arms and legs are tangled and broken, her skin scraped along elbows, knees, and her bare shoulder, and a long, thin piece of white silk is wrapped tightly around her neck.

Crouching next to her, I stare at the hollow sockets where her eyes would have been, and the all-too-familiar nausea burns its way up my throat until Sin grasps my shoulder.

"Look at me, Zoe. Only me."

Snapping my gaze to his, I rein in my panic. "I'm all right. Really."

"No, you are not," he says with a small shake of his head. "But we do not have time for that discussion now." Snapping on a glove, he reaches over the body for a moment. "There. I have lowered her lids. Now look at her and tell me what you see."

Taking a single, slow breath, I return my focus to the woman. "She's in much worse shape than Jacinda. Probably held for longer. Emaciated. Recent, rapid weight loss. Her skin is pale, but there are signs she used to have a tan, so she was probably in the dark for weeks."

A chill starts deep inside me, like a ball of ice in my belly. The snap of padlocks echoes in my ears. Chains. I can *feel* metal bars all around me, and I suck in a sharp breath. "We need to turn her over," I rasp.

"Zoe..."

"No. Now." I wave the crime scene technicians closer. "Do it. Please."

The two mages dressed all in black chant words I don't understand, and the body rises, spins in mid-air, and then settles back onto the concrete. Sin is still wearing a glove, and pulls the woman's dark brown hair off her neck.

The faery tattoo glows in the sunlight, and Sin swears quietly behind me, because drawn on her lower back in what looks like permanent marker is another image. An orange blossom. "He will take another tonight. He is practically gloating about it. Get the body to the morgue," he snaps at the mages. "And tell Dr. Breslin that we need to know exactly how old the tattoo is. Have her run tests on the ligature marks as well."

Standing, I scan the street around us. "Traffic cameras. There's one on the corner, and another at the next block. We need the footage. Maybe we can get a make and model on whatever car was used to dump her."

Sin strips off his glove and tosses it into the small trash bag the techs have set up at the edge of the perimeter. "Come. We need to get to the Bureau. There, we can find everything we need."

WE'VE BEEN at this all day, and we still have no answers. The woman's hands were so damaged, the medical examiner couldn't even pull her prints. She was Fae. At least one hundred and thirty years old.

"The tattoo was done over two weeks ago," Sin says as he drops his phone onto his desk. "And from the weight loss,

Breslin believes she was held for a day, maybe two longer than that."

"How can she tell?" My head is pounding, and I drain my fourth cup of coffee, knowing it's just going to make things worse.

"Some calculation having to do with how dehydrated the woman was when the mark was made." He rubs the back of his neck, then stares up at the ceiling. "The timeline fits with what I can remember. Thorn wants the women weak and terrified before he marks them. Broken enough that the pain will often push them over the edge, but not so broken they do not fight him. He...*enjoys*...the fight."

"Sin..." Reaching across the desk, I brush his fingers with mine. "You didn't do this. Remember that."

"But I did. When I chose not to kill him all those years ago. When I failed to protect—" He jerks his hand away. "I need some air. Do *not* leave the Bureau. Do you understand? You are safe here. He cannot get to you behind these wards."

"Where are you going?" I ask, rushing to follow him as he strides towards the door.

"To see an angel."

I snag his wrist. "He's after you too, you know. Wouldn't we be safer...together?"

Sin steps into the fading sunlight, but then turns, bands an arm around my waist, and pulls me close. "You are safest here. Promise me," he growls then kisses me like he's afraid he's never going to see me again. "You will stay."

"I'll stay," I gasp when he lets go. "The commander's handing out assignments for tonight's stakeout in an hour. Be back by then, okay?"

"I will try."

TWENTY-SIX

Where the hell is Sin? He's been gone for two hours, and we're supposed to head to a seedy bar in the Tenderloin in twenty minutes. The Bureau has a full wardrobe of undercover outfits tailored for each of its agents, and one of the witches helped me choose a tight black skirt, patterned stockings, and a shimmery red tank that dips low between my breasts and leaves next to nothing to the imagination.

Oh, and no bra.

"Stop fidgeting," Amber says as she pins my hair up so delicate ringlets tease my neck. "That spell won't hold the top to your boobs forever, you know. The more you tug at the material, the weaker it gets."

"Great. So I need to worry about a wardrobe malfunction all night?"

The shy witch blushes. She can't be much older than twenty, but her hazel eyes hold wisdom well beyond her years. "Not *all* night. Just maybe after 10:00 p.m. I'm trained in reading auras during interrogation. Physical magic was never my passion."

"Auras?"

Amber steps back and gives me the once over. "Spin for me?"

I try and almost fall over with the three-inch heels I'm wearing. "Don't we have anything more...sensible? How am I supposed to chase after anyone wearing these things?"

"Easy," Amber says with a grin. "Just say the words, 'Feet, don't fail me now.' They'll turn into sneakers."

"Really?" Just when I think I get a handle on this world, there's something new to process. "Feet, don't—"

"Not yet! Otherwise I'll have to reset the whole spell!" Amber shakes her head. "Sorry, I should have said that up front. I forget that you're human. You carry yourself like one of us."

"I have no clue what the fuck I'm doing most of the time," I admit. "But what do you mean 'one of us'?"

"An *other*." The witch frowns and narrows her eyes. "Stand still for a minute, okay?"

"Sure." My skin tingles all over, like something inside me is desperate to escape. It's probably just my desire to get out of these tight clothes, but Amber's stare unnerves me, despite her shy personality. After a full two minutes, I start to fidget again. "Um, Amber? What are you doing?"

The witch flinches, like she forgot I was even here. "Sorry. I was trying to get a read on your aura, and it's...weird." Twirling a lock of blond hair around her finger, she chews on her bottom lip, then swallows hard enough I can hear it. "You're not human, Zoe. I don't know what you are. But you are definitely *not* human. And..." Amber huffs out what might be a laugh. "You knew."

"Suspected," I correct. "And I don't know what I am either. You really have no idea?"

I would do almost anything for answers, and I think Sin has them, but every time we start talking about it, we end up fucking each other blind. So not helpful.

"No. It's like...you're human on the outside, but not the inside." She shrugs. "It's hard to explain. Like, there's this *otherness* deep in your soul, but your body...that's human."

I'm about to press her for more answers when my phone rings. The tight leather skirt has a hidden pocket at the small of my back, and I tap the single earbud in my left ear. "Sin? If you're not back here in—"

"It's Dion." Her voice, usually so bubbly and effusive, holds an edge of strain, and I can hear people talking around her. "I just left my place, and I think the bitch who took Jacinda is following me. I'm scared, Zoe. What do I do?"

"Tell me where you are." I nod at Amber and run—with very small steps thanks to this damn tight skirt—to my desk. "I hear people. You're not alone, right?"

"I'm on Market Street. Ten blocks from Loup Noir. But, Zoe...shit. I don't want to lead her there. And she's getting closer."

"Do not, under any circumstances, talk to her. Do you understand? Don't let her say *a word* to you. Put in your earbuds, blast the music, stay where there are lots of people. I'll meet you outside Macy's in...um...ten minutes."

"Just...hurry. Please."

The Bureau has a pool of cars parked under the building, and I snatch up the keys for a Thunderbird and text Sin from the elevator.

Dion's in trouble. I'm going to pick her up on Market Street, then bring her to the Bureau. Get your ass back here ASAP.

Ten minutes later, my phone buzzes as I double-park

around the corner from Macy's. Sin's name flashes across the screen, but I shove the phone into my pocket. I don't have time for this now. He's just going to yell at me, and in five minutes, I'll have Dion and we'll be on our way back to the Bureau.

My feet are already starting to ache as I turn onto Market Street, but Dion's mane of jet black hair is just barely visible over the rest of the crowd and so I push through the discomfort. She's facing away from me, pretending to window shop at the department store. Thank God.

"Dion!" I say as I reach for her arm.

"Do not say another word," an accented, alluring voice says in my ear. "Your voice belongs to me now."

Panic wraps icy fingers around my heart, and I try to scream, but nothing comes out.

"Give me your phone and your keys," the woman says, and my entire being aches to please her. I can't give her my phone. I need it. And my keys. Dion is only a foot away from me, and her eyes...they're so serene, almost like she's floating on air. Her lips are parted slightly, and she watches the woman behind me. Regina.

The keys slip from my hand, but I don't make a move to pull my phone from my pocket. *Fight. Find your voice and scream your damn head off.*

A tiny, weak sound tickles my throat, and for a second, I think maybe I can fight her. Until Regina turns me around, takes my chin in her long, bony fingers, and pins her cold stare on me. "You will do as I ask, or I will kill the panther by flaying her skin from her body one inch at a time. Give. Me. Your. Phone."

Each word is like a sledgehammer to whatever fight I have left. I'm so tired. And if I give in...everything will be okay. I know it will. Because the old woman is smiling now. Her orange eyes...how did I think they were cold? They're full of tenderness. Understanding. She knows what's best. She'll take care of me.

I slip my phone into her palm, then take out my earbud and drop it on the ground. As Regina slams her foot down on it, something deep inside me knows I've made a terrible mistake. Until she speaks again. "Come now, ladies. Your new master awaits."

With an arm around each of our waists, Regina leads me and Dion to the Thunderbird, tells us to get into the back seat and sit still, and slides behind the wheel.

Fight, Zoe. She's dangerous. She's going to kill you. And Sin.

Squeezing my eyes shut, I try desperately to scream, to move even a single finger. I'm close. So close. The thought of losing Sin—of him caught in Thorn's clutches again—is almost enough to let me break free. But then the Fae bitch turns around with a tiny, odd-looking gun in her hand. "Time to say goodnight."

The dart pierces my neck, and the world turns cold and dark. A tear tumbles down my cheek, and my eyes flutter closed.

As I slip away, I'm so confused, because my inner voice— the one that just a second ago told me I failed—utters one, final thought.

No. You succeeded.

TWENTY-SEVEN

Sin

Zoe is not answering me. Shoving the Bureau doors so hard the walls shake, I call out for her, but I can tell she is gone. As is most everyone else. On their assigned stakeouts across the city.

I should have been here. Should not have driven so far. Why did I not start with a phone call? Sariel, the only watcher I know in the earthen realm, would not answer my questions. He was downright angry at being disturbed, and we battled—physically—for an hour before I bested him and demanded he tell me why the Almighty would torture me like this.

"We cannot claim to know the Almighty's will, demon spawn. If this Zoe truly is your Genevieve reborn, there is a reason she is here. You will have to see it through."

I shove him up against the wall of his shed, lifting him off his feet. "How do I break through the wall built around her memories? At least tell me that!"

The watcher shakes his head. "You cannot. She must do that all on her own."

Stomping through the bullpen, I catch sight of one of the witches. Ashley? Aisha? Amber. "Were you here? When Zoe left?" I snap.

"Yes." Amber rushes over to me, her eyes wide. "She got a call and said something about Macy's on Market Street. Is she in trouble?"

"Thorn has her. I am certain of it." Saying the words aloud is too much, and I brace my hand on Zoe's desk, my world collapsing as I speak.

"What can I do?" the witch asks. "I don't know what she is, Agent Sin, but she's strong. I read her aura before she left, and...she's...something I've never seen before."

I blow out a deep breath, searching for strength. "Zoe is descended from the seraphim. But she can be killed. She has died before. I will not let it happen again." Admitting the truth frees something inside me, and I strip off my leather jacket and my shirt, yank open my desk drawer, and pull out a pocket knife.

"What are you doing, Agent Sin?" The witch takes two steps back, wary, and I offer her a cold grin.

"I'm going to find my partner," I say as I cut two holes in the back of my shirt, another two in the leather jacket, and get dressed once more. "And stop hiding who I truly am."

The witch follows me as I sprint for the parking lot. Now is not the time to bother with human transportation. As soon as I am free of the building, I let out a roar. My wings burst forth, and then there's only air beneath my feet. I bank to the left, seeing Amber's jaw drop open, and take off towards Market Street.

I AM strong enough to glamour everyone within two blocks when I land—thanks to what Zoe and I shared this morning—and I hide my wings until I blend into the crowd. Zoe's scent lingers, so very faint now, but still trackable. It's strongest in front of one of the shop windows, and as I approach, something crunches under my shoe.

Fuck. Zoe's earbud. On the corner, I find her broken cell phone. And on the next block, another concentration of her scent—along with the panther shifter. They used Dion to trap her, and now Thorn has two victims. From Zoe's research, his *final* two victims in this city. In a day, perhaps two, he'll brand them, and not long after, he'll sell their pain and terror for the first time. Let them be ravaged, tortured, tormented by the worst of the otherworld. And he'll drive them slowly insane. Zoe fought before. Can she do it again?

Even if her mind does not break, Thorn will still destroy her body. He will let her be violated, let others break her bones, trap her deep in nightmares she will be unable to escape from. And so much more. All to feed off of her misery.

"Zoe," I whisper as I stare up at the sky, the city lights obscuring the stars. "I will find you. I swear."

Clenching my hands into fists, I call upon all of my strength to hide myself from the world around me and take to the air, returning to the cliff overlooking the Golden Gate Bridge.

"Gabriel! Get your celestial ass down here! Right the fuck now!" The wind howls around me, angry and vicious, and I turn in a slow circle. "Gabriel. I swear if you do not show yourself to me, I will fly up there and pull the feathers from your wings one at a time while you scream for mercy!"

The air stills, and Gabriel's arrival sends me stumbling, but I am ready for him, rolling and beating my wings until I am hovering five feet above him. The energy pulsing from my body lights the darkness, and if I thought I could get away with it, I would toss him over the edge and let his body break against the rocks below. Angels can die in the mortal realm, and though they heal—very quickly—they can still feel pain.

"You have the gall to summon me like this, Sinclair? I could end you in a heartbeat," Gabriel sneers.

"He has her, you piece of shit." The angel's attitude enrages me, and I swoop down and plant my feet in the center of his chest, sending him flying back and skidding on the dirt path for a highly satisfying distance. "You sent a celestial being to the earthen realm with no memory of who she is or knowledge of what she can do. One Thorn has met before. And then you put her right in his path! Tell me why I should not end you right now. You are not immortal on earth, Gabriel. And I am stronger than you by half."

"What are you talking about?" He pushes up on an elbow, raising his other hand in surrender. "Who does Thorn *have* and what kind of celestial being is she?"

"You truly do not know?"

Gabriel is many things. Arrogant, unfeeling, and the least responsible angel I have ever met. But he does not lie.

"No. Of course not. Can I get up now, demon?"

I lower myself until my feet touch the ground, then nod, but I cannot bring myself to offer him a hand.

"I am only half demon. See the wings, asshole?"

"Fine. Halfling," he mutters as he gets to his feet. "Are you going to answer my question?"

"He has Zoe. She is part seraphim. And Gabriel? She is the reason I was able to fight Thorn and Regina centuries ago. Her death gave me the strength to break free from his control and drag the two of them to Hell. I was in love with her. And that incubus bastard killed her right in front of me. If he finds out who she is now? If he already knows? He will not kill her again. He will keep her alive so he can torture her for all eternity."

The archangel's blue eyes widen, and he takes a step back. "Well, fuck."

TWENTY-EIGHT

Zoe

Cold. Damp. Dark. My nose wrinkles, but I don't try to move beyond that. I'm not sure I can. My arms and legs are bent, and I'm folded almost in half. My entire body aches, like I've been in this position for a long time.

The rough stone under my cheek confirms that I'm on my side. My left shoulder throbs. Along with my hip. I can't feel my fingers or my lips.

Images ping around my brain, but they don't coalesce into anything I can understand. A crowd of people. Stormy blue eyes. Black wings. The fires of Hell.

Sin. Oh, shit. Sin. My partner. My lover. My angel.

"You are safest here. Promise me you will stay."

I broke that promise. Broke it for a friend. My first friend. My *only* friend. Dion. Where is she? Her eyes...they were so calm. Serene. Regina forced her to help trap me. And then the Fae took us both.

A tear escapes my shuttered lids and trails across the bridge of my nose. Regina's voice…she spoke to me and stole me away without batting an eye. I couldn't fight her. I wanted to. I tried. But I couldn't.

"The easiest way to get to me would be to go after you."

Do they know? That I'm with Sin? *Am* I with Sin?

The lump in my throat answers the question. Yes. I am absolutely with Sin. I care for him. So much. I think…I think I might even love him. Whatever I am, this *other-ness* inside me knows he's mine as much as it knows I'm his.

Footsteps echo on stone, and I try to prepare myself for what's coming. Pain. Regina stealing my free will. Thorn invading my mind and searching out my greatest fears.

Don't think. Anything. Picture a void. Your mind is nothing but a void.

Behind my lids, I conjure a black hole in space, twisting, consuming all light, all life, everything. Nothing but an endless dark cloud swirling without emotion. Without fear.

A woman screams from far away. Not Dion, but someone else. I can *feel* the woman's desperation. How close she is to breaking completely. The sound echoes around corners and curves, and she begs for her life to end. *"Please. Let me die."*

Her plea stirs something buried deep inside me. A long-ago memory. Another woman, another scream, another time. Trapped in a prison deep underground in the cisterns of Florence, knowing I was sent there to die, to take Thorn with me, but failing. All because of a man whose blue eyes held pain and sorrow and need I couldn't ignore.

If I could move, if I could make any noise at all, I'd let out a wail so loud, so mournful, no one in a hundred miles would be able to ignore it. I remember now. I know why my shoulder and hip ache. Why I smell rust and damp stone. I'm lying on iron bars. Locked in a cage so small, even if Regina's drugs wear off, I won't be able to do more than raise my head.

I can feel the metal clamped around my wrists. The chains binding my ankles. And the weight of millennia of knowledge. Of brief moments of bliss. And endless centuries of pain.

We need you, daughter of seraphim. You failed once. You have another chance. Stop the incubus who calls himself Thorn and his companion and we will release you from your torment.

Tears cascade down my cheeks as everything comes flooding back to me. "How dare you ask me this! The only being I have ever truly loved was consigned to Hell with Thorn and Regina, and you—who claim to be right and just and kind—decided that a fitting punishment for my failure was binding me in the celestial realm, body, mind, and soul, without a single memory of him to comfort me!"

Seraphiel looms over me, glowing with light and power. He does not speak in words, but directly to my mind.

We do not ask, daughter of seraphim. The demon bastard has been returned to the mortal realm to serve the remainder of his sentence. You will do this. We will allow you to see him again, but you will not know him, nor will he know you. Be grateful for this boon. But make no mistake. Your fate does not lie with him. You were made a thousand years ago to put an end to this evil. Created for this one purpose. Until you succeed, you are bound by this duty.

Every cell in my body mourns for what I can never have. I look human. I *feel* human. But I'm not. I was *created* to destroy Thorn, and that's all the seraphim will allow me to do. To be.

Sin...I'm so very sorry. I should have fought harder to remember.

The cage door rattles, and a fist wraps around a chunk of my hair. The rough stone leaves deep cuts in my thighs and arms, and I'd cry out if I could.

"Welcome to your worst nightmare." The raspy voice sends a wave of fear to drown me, and still trapped by Regina's tranquilizer, I can barely force my eyes open to slits. Thorn's pale face swims in and out of focus a few feet away. "Sinclair cares for you. During the long years he toiled for me, through all of my forays into his thoughts and fears, he managed to hide his angelic parentage. But for you...he exposed it without a second thought."

My tongue is thick and unwieldy, but I slur, "He...just wanted...to get me...into bed."

Thorn's laugh sends me back centuries to the caverns under Florence. To the endless days when he toyed with my body and forced his way into my thoughts to find my deepest fears and prey on them.

He doesn't waste a single second. His influence slithers up my spine like a thick fog, blinding my eyes, filling my ears, probing, invading, and searching for ways to break me.

Black void. Nothing but a void.

"A strong one, I see. You are not a shifter. Nor a witch. But you are definitely not human. I wonder. What secrets do you hide? And what will it take for me to discover them?"

The man holding me—one of his human victims—throws me against a wall, and my very human, very fragile body is consumed with pain. I'm descended from angels, yes. Created by them. But they gave me a human body. Human thoughts. Human emotions. All so I would fall into Thorn's trap.

I know who I am now.

My bones will shatter. My skin will tear. Thorn will destroy every human part of me. I can only hope that in the centuries since I was last his prisoner, my mind, the part of me designed to kill him, has strengthened. I just have to remember how I'm supposed to end him.

He stalks towards me, and I manage to curl myself into a ball. My ankles and wrists are still bound, so even if the drugs wear off, I won't be able to fight him. But I have to try. Otherwise, I'll fail once more, and Sin...he'll die along with me.

I CAN'T LIFT my head. There's blood in my eyes, dripping onto the stone floor beneath me. Within minutes of pulling me from the small, iron cage, Thorn had Gregory and another man remove the chains and shackles, but any illusion of freedom was short lived. Too weak to do more than bat helplessly at them, I couldn't stop Gregory from binding my wrists with a thick, plastic zip tie, or the other man from lowering a hook from the ceiling and sliding it between my hands.

The balls of my feet barely scrape the ground, and they cut off my skirt, leaving me in just my skimpy red top and panties. And that's when they started in on me.

The skin of my back burns, that fucking metal-studded whip leaving me bloody from my shoulders all the way down to my thighs. The pain steals my focus so Thorn can delve deep into my mind. Or try to, at least. So far, I've managed to fight him. To at least keep the knowledge of who and what I am hidden away in that dark, swirling void.

I can't scream anymore. My voice is gone. And Thorn is getting frustrated. I have to give him something soon, or I'm afraid he'll push me so hard, so long, that I'll end up giving him *everything*. But I need a break. A few minutes to conjure fears not my own and find a way to trick him. He has Dion, and I can't let her die down here—or let Thorn find a way to use me against Sin.

The incubus bastard grabs a chunk of my hair and pulls my head up so I'm forced to look into his glowing red eyes. "You belong to me now, Zoe Dawes. Tell me about your partner. Tell me how to get to him."

I won't. I can't. Sin is—was—the best part of my entire existence. Of both lives the seraphim gave me. I won't betray him. And I'll do anything to stop Thorn from getting his hands on the man I love.

"Tell me what I need to know, and all this pain stops. Perhaps, I will even let you go," he says, his voice soothing, almost like a balm to my wounds. The constant agony eases, and I sigh. "Yes. You want to feel better, do you not? I can make that happen."

Like Sin with my migraine.

His power pushes into me, a disgusting, vile presence that causes my legs to flail helplessly and my eyes to roll back in my head. *No. I know what you are. What you are doing. It won't work on me, you piece of shit.*

I try to embrace the pain, to use it to focus, but the ephemeral wisps of Thorn's talents wind their way deeper. I can feel them slithering along my nerve endings, turning them off one by one, until half of my body feels like I've just spent a week at a spa while the other half is consumed by burning agony.

He's so close, my breasts push against his broad torso, and his free hand cups my ass. "Give in, Zoe. You are mine now. Why keep fighting? Tell me what you are. Give me Sinclair. You will fetch the highest price at the auction, and you are strong enough to last for years. So much stronger than any of the others. I can give you endless luxuries in exchange for your service. The finest food, a room fit for a queen, even pleasure, if you desire it, but I require your mind in exchange. You know I will have it in the end."

He's right. I may be stronger than I was the last time he had me, but I'm weaker too. Because now I know the truth. I love Sin. And love is the weapon he'll use to destroy me. Unless I end him first. I just don't remember *how* I'm supposed to do that.

Damn Seraphiel and his idiotic idea to block all of my memories.

You will remember when it is time.

The angel's last words to me play on a loop in my head just beyond Thorn's reach. Well, it's time now, you divine bastard.

Frustration churns in Thorn's dark gaze, and the all-consuming agony returns with a vengeance. Digging his fingers into one of the wounds on my back, he laughs when a hoarse, choking cry escapes my cracked lips.

"Your body cannot take much more, my dear Zoe. Nor can your mind. I can feel it."

Drawing on the last of my physical strength, I bring my knee up to catch him in the balls. My demon captor stumbles back with a yelp and doubles over. With his shock comes a less-ening of his power, the tendrils retreating, slinking out of my mind as quickly as they can.

Think, Zoe. Focus.

If I can convince him that he's broken me, he'll make a mistake. Underestimate me. Drop his mental shields. I don't need long. I'm supposed to do something *to* him. Use his own power somehow. I'm so close to remembering.

Think!

Visions of Sin flash through my mind.

I don't want to lose him. Not again.

But I will. I have no choice. This is what I was sent here to do. Sacrifice myself to save so many more. Including Sin.

Thorn straightens, a look of pure, unadulterated rage twisting his already gnarled features. I only have seconds before he's in my head again. I have to hurry. To create a false world he'll believe is real.

Breathing hurts. With every heartbeat, I lose more blood

this human body cannot spare. My greatest fear. I need to show him something he'll believe is my greatest fear. Something that's not Sin.

Vampires. Velma. Her fangs piercing my neck. When I thought I was human, she terrified me. Maybe...if I can just channel that...

"You will pay for that, you pitiful creature," he hisses as he nods at the human men behind me, ready with their whips and canes.

The blows rain down on me harder than before, and Thorn sends every ounce of his power to invade my thoughts. They pierce my defenses, no longer vines, but sharp, jagged rocks that tear through me, searching, until he locks on to the one thought I offer up on a silver platter.

Yes. Take it. Use it. Give me time to remember how to end you.

TWENTY-NINE

I pace outside the massive, gilded doors of the archangels' inner sanctum, waiting for Gabriel to emerge. I hate being here. I cannot do a fucking thing trapped in the celestial realm, but without the angels' help, I will never find Zoe.

When Gabriel pulled me out of Hell to serve the remainder of my sentence on earth, he forbade me from returning to this place, and in order to bring me here now, he bound my celestial powers so the other angels would not see me as a threat.

Because I am. Or would be if I had even an ounce of my angelic strength.

Entering this realm left me defenseless, but my memories, which have been muddled by darkness for centuries, are now as clear as if the events happened yesterday.

Thorn has a schedule. A plan for each of his victims. By my estimation, we have been in the celestial realm for an hour, but time moves differently here. Eighteen hours have passed on earth.

By now, Zoe will have been beaten so brutally, she will wish for death. She will be hungry and cold, dehydrated, and her mind...he will have assaulted her mind time and time again. I hope she is strong enough to resist, but what if she is not? What if she has already broken?

I have to get out of here. Back to the mortal realm where I am at least closer to her. I left the commander a terse message before Gabriel touched my arm and transported me here, so the whole of the Bureau will be looking for Zoe, but Thorn has had centuries to perfect his wards. The mages will not be able to scry for her, the shifters will not be able to track her scent. Only those with the power to see the future have any chance, and they have never been able to find him before. I have little hope they will be able to do so now.

The doors open, and Gabriel strides through, his golden eyes ablaze and his wings ruffled. "Seraphiel is the most infuriating being I have ever met. Even worse than you, Sinclair."

"What happened in there?" I fall into step at his side, unsure where he is going and why, my patience at an all time low.

"He 'has a plan.' One that will see Zoe—Genevieve—whatever you wish to call her—die and take Thorn with her."

Grabbing the archangel's robes, I stop him in his tracks. "No. I will *not* lose her again. I have paid my debt a thousand times over, Gabriel. Two centuries as Lucifer's plaything, another two working for the Bureau... How many souls have I saved?"

"More than your share," he says, the resignation in his tone obvious. "There are those in this realm, Sinclair, who will never allow you back. You know this."

"I do not care if I ever see this realm again. Banish me

permanently. Take my wings if you wish. But do not force me to go through eternity without the woman I love. The woman Thorn's torture stole from my memories."

Gabriel shakes his head and pries my hands from his robes, then stiffens. "Thorn did not take her memory from you, Sinclair. Seraphiel did."

My entire world halts. Turned upside down with those two words. "What?"

The archangel reaches out and lays his hands on me. One over my heart, the other on my forehead. His palms warm, then start to glow, and he whispers, "Remember."

With a violent shudder, I am thrown onto the rocks surrounding Hell. My body has wasted away from my time as Beelzebub's prisoner, and three angels stand over me. Gabriel, Azrael, and Seraphiel.

"Sinclair," Gabriel says, "the Almighty has seen your suffering and has granted you a brief reprieve to speak with us. Tell us why you should be freed from Hell."

"I deserve to burn," I rasp, my throat parched and scarred from two centuries drowning in Lucifer's river of blood and fire. "I should have fought harder. Or ended my own existence so Thorn could not use me to inflict such pain on others."

Azrael frowns. "We are not unreasonable, Sinclair. You helped end many lives, but you did not wield the blades, and you brought the demons down to Hell knowing you would be trapped here with them."

"He killed the woman I loved. She was so strong. She saved me. And he destroyed her."

"She failed because of you," Seraphiel says, his tone edged with judgment. "That is your true crime."

Pushing myself up to my knees, I grab on to Seraphiel's robes. "What do you mean?"

"We created her, demon. A daughter of seraphim. Of celestial origin, though with a human body, a human mind. We sent her to the mortal realm to stop the demon who calls himself Thorn. But you interfered. She fell in love with you. That is why she did not use her power to trap his consciousness in Hell for all eternity. Because it would have consumed her as well. She hesitated, and Thorn seized that opportunity to end her human existence," Seraphiel says, his disgust for me obvious from the sneer curling his lips.

"Her...*human* existence? She lives? In the celestial realm?" Knowing the woman I love is not gone forever gives me a reason to fight. To try to redeem myself, and I clasp my hands together in supplication. "Please. Show her to me. For only a moment. Grant me this one indulgence, and I will never ask for another."

Gabriel snaps his fingers, and a window to the celestial realm opens before me. She is as beautiful as I remember, but there is no life to her. No movement. Her chest does not rise and fall, her eyes, bright as emeralds, do not see.

"What have you done to her?" I cry.

Seraphiel snaps, "She was inconsolable when she returned to us. Because of *you*. Our most powerful weapon against the scum of demonkind, and you made her as weak as any other *human*. So, we have remade her. Trapped her in a prison of her own physical body and wiped her mind clean so that one day, should we ever decide to release her, she might possibly be *useful* again."

The mournful scream rises from deep in my soul, and Azrael grabs me by the arms and hauls me to my feet. "Your time in Hell is over, Sinclair," the angel of Death says. "You will serve out the rest of your sentence in the mortal realm. There are many souls that need your help, and when you have saved enough of them, perhaps, we may allow you to return."

"No," I whisper. "Please, send me back to Hell. I cannot live with the knowledge of what you have done to her."

Seraphiel steps forward, anger burning in his golden eyes. "Then you will live without it." He takes my head in his hands and rips away my memories one by one. Her smile. Her laugh. The scent of her skin. Her touch. The agony is a thousand-fold worse than anything Lucifer has visited upon me over two centuries, and when he is done, I collapse onto the stone, my thoughts jumbled, knowing I have lost *something*, but having no idea what.

Seraphiel arches a brow and gestures to a window into the celestial realm. The frozen image of a beautiful, yet sad woman flashes before my eyes. "Do you recognize her, Sinclair?"

The window shrinks into nothing when I shake my head, and through my confusion, I think...the seraphim smiles. "He is ready."

"Gabriel?" I croak. "Ready for what? Why am I here...?"

The archangel drops to one knee and cups my cheek. "For redemption, Sinclair. It is time to wipe your ledger clean."

"SINCLAIR. LOOK AT ME." Gabriel kneels over me, but we are no longer on the rocks surrounding Hell. The celestial realm is so fucking white, it is almost blinding, and the archangel's face swims in and out of focus.

"How could you let him do that to her? To me?" I shove him, and he lands on his ass a few feet away.

"I had no choice. He outranks me. I swear, I did not know who Zoe was when I first saw her with you." Gabriel makes no move to rise. Smart. I may be powerless in this realm, but my fist still packs a punch.

"Neither did I. Obviously. It was not until we..."

"Fucked?" A dry laugh escapes his lips at my shock. "Being an angel does not stop me from swearing. Or fucking, to be honest. Not that I have in centuries." He shakes his head and fixes his golden eyes on me. "I am the revealer of truth, the bringer of justice, and the interpreter of the Almighty's plan, and I swear to you, Sinclair. *This* is not what I signed on for. I cannot do a damn thing about your banishment to the earthen realm. Nor do I think you want me to. But I *can* help right the wrongs visited upon you and—?"

"Zoe. She is Zoe now, and will be forever more if I can find her in time."

Gabriel rises and offers me his hand. I do not hesitate to take it. He nods as he pulls me to my feet. "We will find her. Save her. And see Thorn and his lover brought to justice once and for all. But we may need a little help."

THIRTY

Zoe

My stomach twists in on itself. I'm so hungry. I don't know how long I've been here. At least a full day. Maybe two. I haven't seen anyone other than Thorn and his human automatons, but I can hear the other women scream.

Dion's cries are the worst. My only friend. She's here because of me. Because Thorn and Regina needed a way to get to me so they could get to Sin. She broke hours ago. I heard it happen. She doesn't curse him now. She begs. Pleads for water. Food. Mercy. If *I'm* starving and so dehydrated my tongue sticks to the roof of my mouth, she must feel so much worse. Her body needs twice as much food as mine, and Thorn isn't giving her anything.

I can't hold out much longer. He'll sell me soon. To some vampire who'll drink my blood, glamour me, or turn me. I can't let him.

So many centuries ago, he auctioned me at least a dozen times. But I was less powerful then. I remember now. What

I'm supposed to do. What I was supposed to do back then. I can get into Thorn's mind in much the same way he can enter mine.

Before, my power was weaker. Seraphiel believed it would take weeks to destroy the incubus. But now, I can trap him in an instant. When I do, my own mind, my entire consciousness, will be shackled to his. My physical body will die, and our souls will be sucked into the void, consumed by the Underworld for all eternity.

Every time he comes for me, I think I should just get it over with. But when Thorn dies, all the women caged down here with me? They'll die too. My connection with Thorn's mind offers me insights I didn't have last time. He holds the keys to the cages and the thick iron gates leading to the surface. Regina won't free them. Her mind is so far gone, so tied to Thorn's, she might not even survive his death.

No one knows where we are. Hell, I don't even know. These tunnels and caverns are old, but not as old as the ones in Italy. Maybe a hundred years? But we're very deep underground. I can't hear any traffic above us. Can't even feel the rumble of cars or trucks or cable cars.

Soft footsteps approach, and light floods this old, crumbling space. Regina. My heart races, and I try to shield my mind, but while I can fight Thorn—for a time—I can't resist the Fae.

"Bring her," she orders, and Gregory unlocks the cell, grabs me by my ankle, and yanks me out. I lunge for his hands, but I'm too weak and slow. "You will not fight back, my dear. You want to obey. To please me, yes?"

No!

"Yes, Regina." My voice holds no emotion, like I'm suddenly two people. The real me, and the mindless shell she controls who only wants to do her bidding.

"Pick her up and follow me," she says, and Gregory throws

me over his shoulder where I hang limp, unresisting, even as my mind struggles to break free from her control.

Regina hums as she walks, a tone I remember from my first life here. "Tie her down next to the other one," she says when Gregory stops moving, and two sets of hands maneuver me face down on a hard, cold block of stone. My wrists and ankles are each bound to a corner, and Gregory presses my left cheek to the rough slab, while someone else buckles a leather strap around my head so tightly, I can't move it at all.

A few feet away, Dion sobs quietly, bound just as I am, and our gazes lock. So much fear and pain churn in her amber eyes. She's in her fully human state, and along with the bloody wounds on her back that mirror mine, there's a strange symbol drawn on her forehead. My powers aren't limited to Thorn, and I reach out and try to connect with Dion's mind.

Oh, God. I understand now. That symbol is a rune to stop her from shifting. She's trapped in her most fragile form, unable to heal herself, unable to use her enhanced strength to fight back. And she's hungry. So hungry.

"Zoe," she whispers. "I'm so sorry..."

"Not your fault." My eyes burn, but I'm so dehydrated, I can't cry.

Thorn's heavy footsteps make us both flinch. "What's happening?" Dion asks, and I don't want to tell her. I can't. If I do, he'll realize there's more to me than he knows.

"It is time for you both to stop fighting," Thorn says, his voice full of anticipation. If I could see him right now, he'd be smiling. I'm sure of it.

The hiss of the blowtorch pulls a whimper from my lips, and the sudden burst of heat in the otherwise frigid room makes goosebumps prickle all over my body.

He waves the faery brand between us, the metal already glowing red hot. "I have perfected this over the centuries, my beautiful toys. Enchanted ink, the right amount of heat. This mark will bind you to me forever."

I should end him now. Stop him from hurting Dion any more than he has. Maybe someone would find her? Sin has to be looking for us. For me. Fuck. I'm so scared.

"See her fear, Zoe," Regina says, her voice close to my ear. "You will feel it, too."

Thorn chuckles, and his influence prods me, tries to connect me with Dion, but he doesn't have to. Regina's words are enough for my own power to take over. I can't focus enough to reach Thorn's mind, and Dion starts to scream.

"Dion," I manage as the blowtorch snaps off and a strange scent fills the room. "Close your eyes. Please."

Regina pulls Dion's dirty black hair off her neck, whispering something into her ear, and Dion squeezes her eyes shut. I can't, though. I have to watch. It's my punishment for failing the last time. For falling in love with Sin and forgetting the reason I was created in the first place. I have to bear witness. I'll honor my only friend by doing what I can to lessen the pain. Regina should have considered her words more carefully.

I'll feel Dion's fear. All of it. By taking a fraction of it away. Just enough that maybe, her broken mind won't shatter into dust.

Her scream is like nothing I've ever heard. Pure hopelessness, agony, and despair. The stench of burned skin and of the enchanted ink makes me want to vomit, but I swallow it down and focus all my energy on her. Thorn holds the brand in place for what feels like an hour, but is probably only a minute or two, and when he pulls the metal away from her body and Dion opens her eyes again, they're glazed over.

I try to sense her, to give her an ounce of comfort, but...it's like she's gone. Like the woman she was no longer exists. Her thoughts...they're all focused on Thorn. On serving him. On being whatever he wants her to be.

Oh, shit.

This mark will bind you to me forever.

He didn't mean we'd be *seen* as his. That others would view the tattoo as a mark of ownership. He meant our minds would be bound to his. The enchanted ink. It augments his power. His will. Fuck. If I'm not strong enough to resist him, this could be my last chance to send his consciousness to Hell.

I was so trapped in Dion's fear and my own panic, I didn't hear the blowtorch turn on again. Didn't smell the burning ink. I gasp for breath, trying to focus my power, but Regina moves my hair aside and leans closer. "Accept his control, my dear. Let him in and stop fighting."

The searing pain consumes me. My muscles struggle against the Fae's compulsion, desperate to thrash, to do something to stop this agony, but my mind floats in a tranquil sea. I can hear myself scream, feel my throat burn.

I was supposed to do something. Something important. Wasn't I? I had a purpose. A reason I was sent here.

"You are mine now, Zoe Dawes. Mine to control. Mine to own. Mine to use as I see fit. And I have so very many plans for you."

Thorn's voice fills my thoughts, and I welcome him in. He's my entire world. I exist only to please him.

Sin

We re-enter the mortal realm outside of Bureau headquarters, and when we reach the bullpen, we're greeted by complete chaos. Kunchin is yelling at the commander, Amber and the other witches are hunched over a map of the city, pouring all of their magic into scrying for Zoe, and everyone else is on the phone, working their contacts.

"Listen up!" I shout, and all eyes turn to us.

"Where the *fuck* have you been?" Commander Eve screeches. "It's been *three days*, Sinclair! For all we know, Zoe's dead already, and you've been doing God-knows-what with…who the hell is this?"

"The Almighty knows exactly what Sinclair has been doing," Gabriel replies, a touch of boredom in his tone. His wings unfurl, and a collective gasp comes from the room. "He's been with me, trying to sort out this mess."

"And you are?" Eve asks.

Straightening his shoulders, Gabriel arches a brow. "I am the Archangel Gabriel, and we have a great deal of work to do. Zoe Dawes is not human, and she has been given a terrible burden to bear. She is the only one who can stop Thorn, but in order to do so, she must die along with him. If you do not want that to happen, you will all listen up and do exactly as I say."

"Sinclair?" Commander Eve reaches out and clasps my shoulder, her talons digging into my torn leather coat. "Tell me you didn't abandon her."

"Did you not hear me, shifter?" Gabriel says.

I wave him off and meet the commander's gaze. "I would never abandon Zoe. She and I…we loved one another once. In another life. One she does not remember. But I do, and I will fight for her until I have nothing left to give."

"And you trust this…archangel?"

My snort earns me a glare from Gabriel, but I ignore him and focus on Eve. "With my life. And Zoe's. He is an asshole, but he is an honorable one."

She takes a step back, pursing her lips. "All right, then."

Sweeping her arm to encompass the whole bullpen, she sighs. "Go ahead, Gabriel. Tell us what to do."

"Sinclair needs to make a phone call. The rest of you? We have to identify at least four—preferably eight—of the worst, depraved, and richest demons in this area and put them under surveillance. The sun sets in what? Three hours?"

Eve nods.

"By then, we must know their whereabouts and be able to take them down on a moment's notice. Thorn and his minions will move the women to another location this evening. Once there, he will collect exorbitant sums of money from a small group of these demons and let them terrorize his victims until dawn. Then, he will return to his heavily warded stronghold. If we do not find them tonight, the chances of rescuing any of them alive diminish greatly."

I cannot stand to hear him speak so dispassionately of Zoe's suffering, so I head for Eve's office and shut the door. The conversation I need to have now requires privacy.

"Sin?" Mad's sleepy voice is full of concern. "It's the middle of the bloody night. What's wrong?"

"I need you, brother. You and your witch."

"Warlock," Killian slurs, clearly listening in. Of course. They're in bed together.

"Fine. Warlock," I say. "Get here in the next three hours, and Killian can call himself whatever he wants. Lord of all magic? King of the witches? Ruler of all creation? I do not give a fuck."

Sheets rustle, and Killian groans as Mad says, "Hang on, Sin."

I do, for all of two minutes, pacing the whole time. I am about to start cursing my own brother's name when he and Killian appear in front of me. Staggering back, I hit Eve's desk and have to brace myself so I do not land on my ass.

"Fuck. When you said 'hang on,' I did not think—"

Maddox pulls me into a tight embrace, and I return the gesture, an unfamiliar burning sensation in my eyes and a lump in my throat. "I know you, Sin," Mad says quietly. "You are not one to ask for help unless there is no other way."

With my brother's arms around me, I cannot hold my emotions in any longer, and a hoarse sob escapes before I can speak again. "There is no other way."

Mad draws back to stare at me. "So, what do you need?"

I turn to Killian. I have never met the man, but Mad discovered video chatting a few months ago, and he was eager to have me virtually "meet" his fated mate. Killian's eyes are kind, but slightly wary.

From my experience, witches are attuned to evil, and Killian will surely sense my demon side.

"Warlock, do you have much experience with transfiguration?"

Killian's brows shoot up, and he whistles. "Transfiguration spells are some of the most dangerous—and unstable—spells in existence. Why do you need to appear to be someone else?"

"Not only me. The three of us...and the archangel Gabriel. We must impersonate four of the most depraved demons in town, infiltrate an auction where the most powerful incubus in all of history sells his victims for sport, and rescue the woman I love."

Rubbing his hands together, Killian offers me a wry smile. "All right, then. Sounds like a bloody good time."

THIRTY-ONE

Zoe

The cold water shocks me awake, and I scream and thrash, tearing the wounds on my back open. But the pain brings a moment of clarity, and I've had few of those since Thorn branded me.

His influence ebbs as two of his men take me by the arms and hold me up while Regina hoses me down. I don't know where my red blouse went. Or my panties. I'm completely naked now, and the frigid deluge makes me shiver. Across the room, Dion sits meekly, dressed in a white silk gown. Her black hair gleams in the light from the Edison lamps around this, the largest cavern I've seen since I was taken.

I'm turned enough for Regina to spray down my back, and now, I can see Dion's eyes enough to try to sense her thoughts. It takes me forever to find any part of her. It's like she's cowering in the back of a massive cave, afraid of the monsters guarding the entrance.

"Hold on for me, Dion. Please."

She flinches once, and her consciousness flares, but quickly fades away. It's enough, though. If I can send Thorn to Hell, maybe she'll be able to fight her way back.

The faery tattoo flares, and I can feel my awareness slipping from my grasp. Fighting him takes everything I have in me, and my knees buckle.

The next thing I know, I'm wearing a dress identical to Dion's, sitting next to her with another woman, the girl with frizzy hair who disappeared the night Sin went to Loup Noir. I don't risk turning my head to look into her eyes. Not yet.

A fourth woman is being hosed down now, and a fifth stands stock still waiting for her turn. The auction won't take place down here. They'll move us to another location. With only three human men in his thrall, plus Regina, there's no way Thorn will risk us being awake and aware. He'll drug us, I'm sure.

"This looks like a fresh needle mark. Made less than twelve hours before she died." Dr. Breslin's words rattle around in my head. Of course.

The drugs will make it harder for me to resist his influence. But once he hands me over to one of his *customers*, he'll relinquish control. If he doesn't, he won't be able to feed off of my terror. That will be my best chance.

I know his mind. I've been in it before. But can I latch on to his consciousness from a distance?

He's had me for days. I'm so physically weak, I can barely stand. I won't be able to fight off another demon to get to him.

A soft touch to my pinky draws my focus, and I lower my eyes to see Dion's hand pressed to mine. She's still in there. Fighting along with me.

I have to preserve my strength, but I can't let Dion think she's alone. Snagging her finger, I squeeze lightly, and the corner of her mouth twitches for a second.

I'll get her out of this. I can do this one thing. Save *one* person, even though I'll lose myself in the process. Taking a risk, I meet her gaze.

"When you get free, find Sin. And tell him I loved him."

A single tear rolls down her cheek. She knows now. I don't intend to survive this. I can't. But she will. As will Sin.

Sin

Darkness blankets the area around an old, abandoned power house at Hunter's Point Naval Shipyard. The lights from the city are as bright as any moon, but they fade into darkness around the multi-story cement structure.

"Well, that's a rubbish spell if I've ever seen one," Killian mutters. "No finesse. It's like he's not even trying."

At my side, Mad stifles a snort. "For a witch who couldn't cast a spell a year ago, you're terribly judgmental now, love."

"I could cast any spell I wanted," Killian replies. "I just didn't want to blow up the entire world in the process."

"This is supposed to inspire confidence?" The two of them banter endlessly, the kind of back and forth that only comes from mutual love and respect. I want that. I ache for it. With Zoe. I hope to all that is holy I will get that chance.

"My witch can do anything." Mad presses a kiss to his mate's cheek and then straightens his jacket. "Including turn me into an Asmodeus demon. For at least a few hours."

The Bureau came through. Sixteen demons identified, tracked, and monitored for hours until seven of them started heading for Hunter's Point. It took every agent to bring down four of them. Two Asmodeus demons, known for their unbridled lust and insatiable sex drives, a half-Fae, half-incubus, and a direct descendent of the Lord of Greed himself, Mammon.

Killian draws symbol after symbol in the air, then starts chanting softly to himself. Magic swirls around us, and my skin prickles as the spell takes hold. When I look at our group, I cannot help but gape. Mad and Killian are nearly twins. Reddish skin, well-muscled bodies, mostly naked save for tight, black trousers that end mid-calf and highlight their wide feet.

"Ew," Mad says, but even his voice has changed. Deep and rumbling, it matches his bulk.

Gabriel reaches up with long, claw-like fingers to touch the two sets of horns protruding from his forehead. "If we are not successful, I trust you will be able to wipe all memory of this moment from our minds, warlock."

"If this all goes pear-shaped, we'll be dead, so I doubt that'll be an issue." Killian shrugs his now massive shoulders, and I stare down at my hands. Still mostly human in appearance. Fae can take many forms, and the small wings protruding from my shoulder blades feel foreign, but my mouth has not changed shape, my vision is unaltered, and when I take a step towards the power station, I feel...almost myself.

"This is not what I imagined we'd be doing today, luv," Killian says as he and my brother fall into step behind me.

"What? Saving the world?" Mad chuckles, but it sounds more like a roar than a laugh. "Better than what you had planned for us. Cleaning out the basement?"

"At least in the basement, we'd have been alone," Killian says. "And naked."

Mad sighs. "Bloody hell. Sin, this had better work."

It will. It has to. Or I will not survive it.

WE'RE MET at the door by the missing human, Gregory. "Your names?" His voice holds no inflection, and the dead, haunted look in his eyes is one I know well. There is nothing left of his mind. No independent thought. He broke long ago, and his consciousness belongs only to Thorn.

Mad and Killian go first, and Gregory holds out a small tablet. "Your fee is thirty thousand dollars, paid up front. Enter your transfer details now."

We prepared for this, and Mad signs away a chunk of my fortune, as do I, followed by Gabriel, and finally, we are allowed to pass. Once inside, Mad and his warlock make their way to the front of the room, with Gabriel heading left. I weave my way through a small gathering of other demons—most only here to watch—until I am positioned to the right of a raised dais that remains suspiciously devoid of all activity.

"There is ancient magic at work here," Killian says quietly over the comms devices we each have in our ears. He throws his arm around Mad, and the two of them stumble purposely towards the empty space until they appear to hit an invisible wall, then get themselves under control and step back. "If this Thorn is here with the women, they're behind this ward."

"Keep your voices down," Gabriel hisses. "If we show our hand too early, this will all be for naught."

He needn't have worried. Seconds later, the ward vanishes with a gust of wind, and all eyes turn to the front of the room.

Fuck. Zoe stands immediately to Thorn's right, with Dion, the panther, on his left. Six women in total. Including the one I failed to save at Loup Noir. They are all dressed in identical white silk sheaths that leave nothing to the imagination, and wear the same blank stares.

My heart, which I did not think could shatter any further, turns to dust. We wasted too much time in the celestial realm. Three days? How could I expect her to fight him for three days? I killed her. I did not break her mind, but I killed her all the same.

I can almost *hear* each piece of my soul crumble and fall until Thorn starts to speak, and his voice...it still holds sway over me, even after all these centuries.

"Welcome all," he says with a flourish of his hand and a small bow. "This will be a night you will surely remember for all of your existence. Six of you—well, seven—" he says with a nod at Mad and Killian, "—have procured the use of my exquisite creations. In just a few moments, I will release their minds, and you will have until dawn's first light to do *anything* you desire with them and *to* them. I have only one rule. They must still be alive when you return them to me."

A massive demon with deathly pale skin stretched so tightly over his muscles I am surprised he can move, huffs in displeasure, but the rest of the crowd is silent.

"Those of you who were not fortunate enough to garner a winning bid may observe. Individual playrooms are on the upper floor, all warded to prevent the women from escaping. My mark," Thorn says as he grabs Zoe's arm and spins her around, "is what will stop them, so please do not destroy it."

Rage consumes me, drowning out all other thoughts, all emotion. He branded her, beat her, and bloodied her. The gown's plunging back reveals the wounds, barely healed, and in the lights bathing the dais, the faery tattoo shimmers and flares to life.

Turning her to face the crowd once more, Thorn grins, revealing his sharp, yellowing teeth. "Who shall be the first?" he calls out.

Zoe raises her head a fraction of an inch, and her hands clench into fists. She is fighting him, and my rage turns to hope. If there is anything of her left, our plan may still work.

A dozen Bureau agents wait outside the building, and I am

about to call for the attack when Zoe's gaze locks onto mine. A hoarse sob escapes her throat, and Thorn pulls her against him as he scans the room.

"Ah, Sinclair, my old friend. I hoped you would join us. Where are you?"

Zoe's bright green eyes have gone dull, her mind once again under Thorn's control. He will root through her memories, caring little what damage he does, until he sees me as she did. I cannot let her suffer any more than she already has.

"Right here." Pushing through the crowd, I stand only feet away, and Regina quickly appears at my side.

"You will not move," she says, her voice as sweet and compelling as I remember. But my love for Zoe breaks the mental chains she attempts to use to bind me. I have a reason to fight now, and I will die before I give in. Before I lose Zoe.

"Fuck off." I let my wings unfurl, send her flying back into the crowd, and sprint towards Thorn until the silver blade in his hand catches the light.

"Not another step, Sinclair, or I will destroy her." The tip of the blade presses to Zoe's breast, and blood stains the white silk.

Zoe cries out, first a tiny whimper, then a scream, and with one final, long look at me—one filled with sorrow, determination, and love, her eyes roll back in her head, and she and Thorn crumple to the ground.

THIRTY-TWO

Fusing my consciousness to Thorn's is the most painful thing I have ever experienced. Far worse than the centuries I spent being remade, time I now remember in excruciating detail.

Seraphiel kept me locked in a prison of my own body while he chipped away at my mind one memory at a time. Each one was precious to me, and though I'd been human for only weeks at that point, I remembered what it was to *live*. Until he took that as well.

Now, I will never live again. The descent to the Underworld is dizzying and faster than I anticipated. I hold Sin's face in my mind—what is left of it anyway—for Thorn has had centuries of life lending him strength, where I have not even managed two years.

He struggles against my hold, cursing me, trying to tear my consciousness to shreds, but while whatever made me...*me*...will soon be gone, I was created for this purpose alone. I have the power to hold on long enough for the fires of Hell to surround us.

They're getting closer now, and I marvel that I can feel them as if I still had a physical body. Opening my eyes, I gasp as I see that somehow, I do. In a way. We're more like ghosts now. Echoes of what we once were. The first tongues of flames lick along our feet, and Thorn screams.

All around us, there's nothing but endless suffering, and I can sense Lucifer's presence looming just ahead. The devil laughs, almost gleeful. "How nice to see you again, you pathetic twat. You escaped right under my nose the last time, but now...you will be forever mine."

"I freed myself once. I will do it again," Thorn hisses, and I tighten my hold on his immortal soul.

"Not if I have anything to say about it," I manage.

"You are nothing but a weak, pathetic human with a single touch of the divine, bitch."

Lucifer chuckles again. "Hardly. She is a daughter of seraphim, and the bond she formed with you is unbreakable."

Fiery shackles lock Thorn's ephemeral wrist to mine, and I take a small measure of joy—the last I'll ever feel—from his scream.

The devil reaches for his pitchfork—I'd thought that was a myth until now—and stabs Thorn through the heart. The agony is like nothing I've ever felt, but I take solace from knowing that at least I saved the man I love.

Sin

"No! Zoe!"

Bureau agents stream into the facility, but I have eyes only for the woman I love. Her skin is ashen, her eyes open and staring, and when I pull her into my arms, I know.

She's gone.

Her heart no longer beats, and it is little comfort knowing that Thorn died along with her. I kick his body out of the way so I can sit with her and plead with the Almighty to do *something*.

Fingers dig into my calf, and I tear my gaze from Zoe's lifeless eyes. Dion is on her knees, tears glistening on her cheeks. "She knew she wouldn't survive, Sin. She asked me to tell you...she loved you."

Too weak to hold herself up any longer, Dion collapses, and Mad comes to her aid, helping her into the arms of one of the Bureau's mages as I scan the room. The two human men are dead. As is Regina. I broke her neck when I batted her away, and whatever immortality she possessed must have been tied to Thorn. The other women on the dais are all still alive, though two of them are so far gone, they barely respond to the mages at all.

"Sinclair." The commander stands over us, eyes glistening. "Tell me she isn't dead."

"She sacrificed herself to save the others," I manage over the lump in my throat. "And to save me."

"But how?"

Gabriel joins Eve, followed by Killian and Mad. I can't look at any of them. Only Zoe. Her skin is cold now, her lips blue, and I cannot stop my tears from falling as I hold her close and tell her over and over again that I will love her until my last breath.

The archangel is saying something. Explaining, I think. But I care little. Until Mad claps his hand on my shoulder. "Sin. Did you hear what Killian said?"

Blinking hard so I can see the warlock's face through my anguish, I shake my head.

"If Gabriel is correct—"

"Of course I'm correct. I'm a fucking angel, you British bastard."

"Shut it," Killian snaps before returning his focus to me. "Zoe bound her consciousness to that arse's and descended into the Underworld, yeah?"

"Yes," I say softly.

"And there are only two ways out of Hell. Either Lucifer decides to let you go, or an angel comes to retrieve you."

"An angel can only retrieve a physical being," I say, almost too weary to continue this conversation. It will not bring Zoe back to me, and I wish to be alone with my grief. "That is how Gabriel and the others freed me, but it will not work with a soul. That requires a tether to a consciousness in the earthen or celestial realm, and more power than has ever been amassed before."

Mad kneels next to me, pride shining in his eyes. "You don't know my mate, Sin. He brought me back to life. And he knows more about magic than any witch of this age."

"Warlock," Killian says with a sigh. "Why can't people get it through their heads..." Throwing up his hands, he makes an exasperated groan. "Never mind. Sin, many years ago, my mentor gave me a book of ancient spells and told me to memorize them because one day, I'd need them. Most were rubbish, but one..." He runs a hand through his dark hair, then looks to Gabriel. "If you can gather enough angelic power, I think I can create the tether."

"How much do you need?" Gabriel asks.

"As much as you can give me."

The archangel steps into the center of the now empty

room. Only the commander, Mad and Killian remain with me and Zoe's body.

"Brace yourselves." Gabriel closes his eyes, unfurls his wings, and raises his hands in supplication. "This...is going to hurt."

For several moments, nothing happens, but then the air in the room thickens, and the building's walls shake, bits of concrete falling from the ceiling. Killian shields us, his magic sending the shards bouncing away harmlessly, until power explodes in a massive circle around Gabriel, blowing the entire top floor of the power house away so the night sky and a full moon illuminate a cloud of dust.

When it settles, we gape at the sight. Six angels, including Michael himself, stand with Gabriel, and the archangel I once considered the biggest asshole in the celestial realm glances around with a smug grin. "Is this enough...*warlock?*"

Killian staggers to his feet and wipes a bit of blood from his ear. The pressure change when *one* angel appears is enough to damage a human eardrum. Six? I am amazed any of us are still alive.

"Not bad, angel. Not bad at all."

***

I REFUSE to let go of Zoe. "If I maintain contact with her physical body, it will strengthen my consciousness," I say, and Killian frowns.

"It might, but it will be harder for me to pull you back along the tether if you fail."

"You assume I am going to fail."

"This plan is as daft as they come," the warlock says. "It will take a miracle for you to be able to separate her from Thorn down there, and that's assuming you can even *find* her. I know I can pull you back to this realm with the tether. The rest...? It's a bloody crapshoot."

I reach for my brother's hand and hold on tight. "Mad, I have to do this. You understand why?"

He touches his forehead to mine. "I would do the same thing for Killian. And Sin, I forgive you."

Commander Eve clears her throat. "Will someone explain to me why Sinclair appears to be saying his final goodbyes?"

I meet her gaze. "Because if I cannot rescue Zoe and bring her back with me, I am going to release my hold on the tether and let Hell take me."

"You will do no such—"

"I will, Grayson. This is my mate. My one true love. We found each other in *two* lifetimes. Do you have any idea how rare that is? I will not lose her again. If I cannot be with her in this realm, I will suffer alongside her for all eternity."

"Then you damn well better get her back," she says. "Because you and I are going to have some serious words about following Bureau procedures when you return, and if you stay in Hell, I just might come down there after you to rip you a new one." Her voice cracks, and she stalks away, leaving only my brother, his mate, and the angels to watch over me.

"Are you ready?" Killian asks.

I caress Zoe's cheek, my tears, which I cannot seem to stop, giving her an ethereal glow, almost as if her angelic origins are shining through. "I will find you, my pearl. My one and only. Hold on. I am coming."

Meeting Killian's gaze, I nod. "Do it."

The warlock draws a series of runes in the air, and they glow with his magic, like fireworks hovering six feet above the ground. He begins a low chant, his words too soft for me to hear, and the angels form a circle around us and join hands.

A thunderous crack is accompanied by a light so bright, it burns my eyes, and Killian shouts, "Sin! Get ready!"

The sensation of one's soul being sucked from one's body is indescribable. There is pain, of course, but also a loss so great, it dwarfs all but the most intense grief. It is nothing compared to what I felt when Zoe sacrificed herself, and I lean in to the physical and mental anguish, welcoming it, and letting go of my physical form so I can fall into the depths of Hell and rescue the only woman I have ever loved.

THIRTY-THREE

When I brought Thorn and Regina to Hell centuries ago, I held each of them in one arm and flew. For an angel, the Under-world is accessible only through a single passage on the way to the celestial realm. A detour, if you will. At least in corporeal form.

Now, I am nothing but consciousness, yet, as I watch myself sink into the fiery depths, I can still *see* my body. Not the distinct, solid form it has in the remains of the power station, but a hazy, diffuse existence, as if I am phasing in and out.

The angelic tether glows around my waist, and I run my fingers over it, feeling the power of those I never thought would help me again.

Fire surrounds me, setting my clothing ablaze, another surprise. How can I feel my leather jacket burning? The soles of my boots melting? My socks bursting into flames?

This is Hell, and anything is possible here.

I grit my teeth against the pain that is only in my mind, but feels every bit as real as when I offered my body to Lucifer in exchange for keeping the most vile demon in existence prisoner. The Devil owes me for his failure. One soul. Zoe's. And I intend to collect on the debt.

Until I am faced with the sight—and sounds—of my failures. The women I let die, everyone Thorn drove mad with pain and fear to feed his insatiable appetites. They surround me, and it matters little that I know they are not real.

I falter, crying out in anguish as I press my hands to my eyes so I will not have to see. The images are too vivid. Too real. The stench of the underground caverns in Florence. Human waste. Blood. Terror. The feel of the lash against my back. Of the chains he used to bind me, and the iron bars beneath my feet.

Thorn's consciousness will be somewhere in the flaming river of blood. As I reach Phlegethon's banks, I fall to my knees and beg for strength. I burned in these very waters for so long, and now, I feel as if I'm drowning yet again. Doubts creep into my thoughts. I failed Zoe twice. Perhaps I am not strong enough, not worthy of her love, of happiness, of any peace. My crimes are legion, and while I have paid for them a thousand times over, is it enough? Will it ever be enough?

The glow of the tether is fading. Killian warned me he did not know how long he could hold the spell. I should release it— and him. As I fumble for the knot, a desperate wail carries over the roar of the flames.

Zoe.

She is close. And her soul has not yet succumbed to madness. For when that happens, she will stop screaming.

I focus all of my energy on the sound of her voice and dive into the flames.

Zoe

Whatever I imagined before I pulled Thorn with me to the Underworld, the reality is infinitely worse. At my side, he writhes and curses the devil, fighting against the chains weighing us down, submerging us up to our necks in a river of fire and blood. My throat is raw, and my skin—despite my lack of a physical body—burns, regenerates, and burns again. Ash clogs my lungs, and when Thorn tires of railing at Lucifer, he turns to me, beating me, choking me, and trying to force my head beneath the surface.

It does not matter what he does. This is where we will spend eternity. But he can hasten my descent into madness, and despite how badly I wanted to live, I know I never will again. Seconds in Hell feel like a century, and when I close my eyes, I relive every moment this demon spent feeding off of others' fear.

"Zoe!"

"No," I wail. "Do not torment me with thoughts of him! This...this is enough. I accept my guilt. My sentence. I cannot endure a memory of true happiness!"

Lucifer is an asshole. Why else would he send me a vision of Sin racing for me, love shining in his blue eyes.

"Zoe, take my hand," the vision says, and oh, how I want to. But this is a trick. A way for the devil to make my endless torment so much worse. "Zoe, my precious pearl, please. We have little time. I can save you!"

Next to me, Thorn tries to push me under again, and this time, I don't fight him. The crackling, flaming waters swallow me, and the agony increases a hundred fold. Until a hand plunges beneath the surface and grabs my arm, pulling me up so I'm face to face with the memory of my one true love.

"You have a gift, Zoe. One that lets you see the truth in a person's eyes. Look into mine now. *See* me," the vision of Sin begs.

I can't help it. I want so much to see him again that I do as he asks. Oh, my God. He's here. His soul is in Hell, half-submerged in the flaming waters with me. "Sin?"

"Yes, my love. My Zoe. Give me your hands. There is still time."

I show him the fiery shackle that locks me to Thorn. "I can't. There's nothing that can free me, Sin. Even if there were, we can't leave. You should know this better than anyone…"

Sin grabs our wrists and pulls, but that only tightens the flaming metal and draws a hoarse whimper from my throat.

Rage consumes my lover's eyes, and a red ring surrounds the sapphire blue. He's weakening. "If you have a way out, Sin, take it. Now. Before it's too late."

"Lucifer!" he shouts. "You know she does not deserve this! Do something! I have the angels on my side. The Almighty's blessing. If you stand in my way…"

With a crack, the devil himself appears before me and hefts his pitchfork. "I am not a complete twat, Sinclair. But you cannot deny me a modicum of fun." With a grin, he swings the weapon down, and the manacle around my wrist shatters into dust. The chains wrapped around my legs fall away, and I lunge for Sin, clinging to his neck.

"Thank you," Sin says, and Lucifer nods.

"Go. I cannot hold him here for long without her. Close the portal before he can follow, burn his body in the earthen realm, and he will never be able to escape again."

Sin reaches down and tugs on what looks for all the world

like a glowing rope tied around his waist. We start to rise, slowly at first, but picking up speed with every passing second.

I can feel his pain along with my own. We're still burning, still hearing the screams of the damned, but there's a pinprick of light high above that's getting brighter.

"How?" I whisper, holding on with all the strength I have left.

Sin presses a kiss to my blistered lips. "Love."

I can see the earthen realm. Our lifeless bodies intertwined with Sin's arms around me. But there's more. Angels. Gabriel, Ariel, Cassiel, Raphael, Azrael, and even Michael. Standing together, hands clasped, wings like beacons in the night sky. And another. One who looks so much like Sin he can only be his brother.

As Sin grasps Gabriel's hand, Thorn lets out a roar and wraps his arms around my legs. It's so sudden, and we're moving so fast, that I'm ripped away from Sin before I can scream.

"Zoe!" Sin dives down and grabs both of my hands. I'm being torn apart, my soul split between life and death, and I can do nothing but focus on the pure, raw grief in Sin's eyes.

Until Gabriel lifts off from the ground in the earthen realm and flies through the portal. His wings start to burn, but he doesn't seem to notice or care. When he reaches me, he hauls his fist back and slams it into Thorn's face. "They have paid their debt, you pathetic piece of shit. But you have not even started."

The demon falls, and Gabriel wraps an arm around my waist and helps us back to the edge of the portal. "Do not fear," he says quietly. "This next part...is not easy."

Everything around me fades into darkness, but though I'm terrified this has all been an illusion, I can still feel Sin holding me, and I give in to the overwhelming desire to rest.

THIRTY-FOUR

I am shivering. After burning in the fires of Hell, everything around me feels frigid. I cannot see, but voices echo close by. What are they saying? The words are muffled. A cacophony that makes no sense.

Other sensations start to return. A tingle in my hands and feet, a softness against my chest. Breath.

Under my fingers, drying blood, sticky and cool. Wounds not yet healed. Zoe's, not mine. The softness of her hair. Her scent.

"Sin." Mad's voice cuts through my jumbled thoughts. "Open your eyes, Sin."

"Zoe," I whisper. The single word takes all of my strength, but if she is not here with me, I do not want to go on.

"She's alive. But she hasn't moved yet, except to breathe. You have to help her, brother."

Forcing my lids open, I thank God the angels are no longer lit up like the sun. Gabriel kneels next to Mad, his wings half burned away, and Michael supports Killian as he staggers over to us.

"You brought her back," Gabriel says. "But a soul ripped from the body often needs convincing to return. She won't believe anyone but you."

Mad and Gabriel carry us over to a wall, propping me up with Zoe cradled in my arms. Her white gown is covered in blood, and she's so very pale. But a tinge of pink colors her cheeks, and her chest rises and falls slowly.

"Zoe? Can you hear me, my love?" From the first day we met—for the second time—I have been able to sense her emotions, but now, I feel nothing. Only an empty void.

Placing my hand over her heart, I focus all my remaining strength on my love for her. "Feel me, Zoe. Hear me. Come back to me. We escaped Hell. Together. I will not lose you now."

She shudders, and a burst of fear hits me square in the chest. Her fear. I would do anything to take it away from her, and I will, but for a brief second, I relish it, because it means her soul is fighting its way back.

"I love you, my pearl. Only you. Always you. I will never fail you again. I swear it." Leaning down, I brush a kiss to her lips, and her fear ebbs, a small kernel of hope deep inside growing steadily stronger. "Fight, Zoe. Fight for us." Another kiss, and this time, her lips part for me.

She is so very weak, but she gives me what little power she has.

I pull back, refusing to take what I know she cannot spare, and find her eyes open and a soft smile curving her lips. "Sin," she whispers. "You...came for me."

"I will always come for you."

"We're...safe?"

"Yes. He could not escape with us. Gabriel made sure of that."

"M'kay. Gonna pass out now," she manages, then goes limp with a deep sigh.

Staring up at my brother with tears in my eyes, I want—no, I need—to ask him for one more favor. But he has done so much for me. He and his mate. And I do not deserve anything else.

Though we have spent most of our lives apart, Mad can still tell what I am thinking with only a look. He takes Killian's hand, and the warlock draws strength from the touch and nods. "Together," Killian says. "We can do it."

Mad smiles at me, and though he is centuries younger than I am, he is wiser by the same measure. "We'll get you home, Sin. Both of you. Rest now. Together."

I close my eyes and nestle Zoe more securely in my arms. We found one another again, and this time, I will never let her go.

* * *

Zoe

Awareness returns a breath at a time. I don't want to wake up. What if this is all a dream? Or really...a nightmare? But Sin's delicious scent surrounds me. Fresh. Clean. Hints of spice and oak and sunlight, and as I take a deeper breath, soft sheets whisper over my naked skin.

"Zoe." His deep voice rumbles through me, and I realize I'm practically lying on his chest. "You are safe. In my bed."

"The sheets kind of gave it away. You have the best sheets."

He chuckles and brushes a tangle of curls from my cheek. "I see it takes only a day of sleep to restore the sharp wit I love."

"A day?" Opening my eyes, I take in the room. It's not quite dawn, the sky beyond the windows just starting to lighten in the east. "It's been an entire day?"

"Yes." Sin tips my chin up, and I find his eyes. Only a hint of sapphire blue surrounds his pupils. The rest of his irises are blood red. "But I would have waited for you for weeks if that is what you had needed."

"You're hungry."

"I am always hungry for you, Zoe. But you are still too weak to feed me. Do not fear. We have time."

"Um, not from your eyes we don't." I push myself up on an elbow and hiss in pain as the wounds across my back pull taut. "Shit."

"Lie still," he says and eases me down again. His hand cups the back of my neck, and a dull ache brings back the memory of Thorn invading my mind. Trying to break me, to force me to betray the man I love. The man who saved me. Tears burn my eyes, and I reach back to finger the raised edges of the brand.

"Killian tried his best, but you will bear the mark for the rest of your life," Sin says, sorrow lacing his tone. He holds out his arm, and his own brand has returned, as clear as I remember it from my first life so many years ago. "As will I."

"You're not going to burn it off again?" I trace his tattoo, the skin around it still burned, but the mark itself unblemished.

"No. Because if not for what we both endured, we would not be here now. We would not have found one another. Fallen in love. Twice." Sin brushes his lips to my cheek, and I turn my head, kissing him and offering all that I am.

The energy flowing between us makes my nipples tighten and floods my core with a desperate need so strong, it overrides all rational thought.

"Zoe," Sin protests when he finally manages to break off our kiss, "you must rest."

"I need you." Cupping his cheeks, feeling the rasp of

several days of stubble against my palms, I meet his gaze. "The last time we made love, I didn't know who I was. Who I'd been. I do now, and I need this—need *you*."

"I will not be responsible for causing you more pain," he says.

"Then give me what I need. Make me yours and let me claim you as mine knowing exactly who I am."

"Who are you?" His lips brush my ear, then trail down the curve of my neck. "You were stripped of all that you once were. Now, you can choose. Who do you want to be?"

Sparks of pleasure race through me when he pinches my nipple, and his teeth score along my collar bone to the hollow of my throat.

"Zoe. I'm Zoe Dawes. Because that's the name I had when I realized I loved you. That's the name I had when I remembered loving you once before. And I will never be anyone but Zoe Dawes ever again."

Sin positions himself between my legs and stares up at me. "Are you certain?"

"I have never been more sure of anything in two lifetimes. Make love to me, Sin."

He kisses up the inside of my thigh, over my mound, and back down, and with every touch of his lips to my body, I feel stronger. More grounded. More...*me*.

"I love you, Zoe," he says after a light flick of his tongue to my clit. "I did not think myself capable of feeling...*anything* ever again, but you changed that."

He doesn't give me a chance to respond, returning his focus to my pleasure. With each taste, our bond strengthens, as does my desperate need for release.

"Sin," I gasp, so close to the edge I feel like I could fly, "I want you inside me when I come."

He growls, moving so quickly, the room blurs as he flips our positions so I'm straddling him, his cock nudging my entrance. "You are in control, Zoe. Do with me what you will."

The thrill of his words is nothing compared to the feel of him when I sink down and let him fill me. Pure power and strength swirl around us as I thrust my hips, and his fingers dig into my ass, urging me to ride him harder, faster.

With my gaze firmly locked on his, I link our fingers on either side of his head, and my nipples scrape against his chest, taking me higher than I've ever been. But I have to hold on. Because when I fly, he's coming with me.

"Zoe. Tell me," he says, each word escaping on a grunt. "And then let go."

"I love you. You're mine. And I'm yours." With more strength than I should have, I slam into him and scream his name.

"Sin!"

EPILOGUE

For almost a week, Zoe and I spend most of our time in bed or wrapped in one another's arms on the sofa watching old movies, talking, or testing the physical limits of how often two celestial beings can have sex.

Mad and Killian are to visit tonight. Along with Dion, Kunchin, and Gabriel, though Zoe forbade him from materializing inside the apartment and injuring her ear drums again. The archangel has apparently decided his lack of time spent in the mortal realm is a detriment to his celestial duties, and has been galavanting around the United States.

Though a part of me wants to hold on to the hatred I carried for him for centuries, I cannot. He saved us in the end at great risk to himself. An angel's wings can only be damaged by Hell's fire, and he can no longer fly. He will again, but it will take some time.

"Are you certain about this?" I ask when Zoe turns away

from the mirror and smoothes her hands down her emerald green sweater. "You do not need to live the life someone else chose for you any longer. No one would blame you if you decided not to return to the Bureau."

"The Bureau gave me you," she says. I start to protest, and she silences me with a swift, passionate kiss. "But that's not all. It gave me my first true friends. The first ones I was ever allowed to choose for myself."

Dion and Kunchin. The yeti has visited three times, twice bringing Zoe's favorite doughnuts—glazed old fashioned—and though Dion only felt up to leaving her apartment for the first time this morning, she and Zoe have talked on the phone every day.

"You have a brilliant mind." I trail a knuckle along her jaw and brush my thumb over her lips. "And I could not imagine taking on another partner ever again, but I would do so if you needed. I hope you know that."

"I do." Wrapping her arms around my waist, she rests her cheek over my heart. "This is what I want, Sin. All of it. This job. This name. This *life*. With you."

"Then, shall we get on with it? The commander may go easy on *you* for a few more weeks, but if we're even a single minute late for our shift, I am likely to face her wrath."

"Just promise me one thing," Zoe says with a smile as I help her on with her jacket.

"What is that?"

"Keep your speed demon tendencies under control in the car. I may have been created by the seraphim, but my stomach is all human."

I arch a brow. "My love, I am a *sex* demon. Or have you already forgotten how I woke you this morning?"

Her laugh is my second favorite sound.

The first? Her screaming my name when I make her come. I may have my wings, but I am, after all, only half angel.

The End

ACKNOWLEDGMENTS

Special thanks go out to Kim, who helped me with a last minute change that made the book so much better, and for all those who forgave me for disappearing for the last week I was working on Storm of Sin when I couldn't concentrate on anything else!

And more than anything, for my readers. I hope you love Storm of Sin as much as I do. Thank you for reading. <3

ABOUT THE AUTHOR

I've always made up stories. Sometimes I even acted them out. I probably shouldn't admit that my childhood best friend and I used to run around the backyard pretending to fly in our Invisible Jet and rescue Steve Trevor. Oops.

Now that I'm too old to spin around in circles with felt magic bracelets on my wrists, I put "pen to paper" instead. Figuratively, at least. Fingers to keyboard is more accurate.

Outside of my writing, I'm a professional editor, a software geek, a singer (in the shower only), and a runner. I love red wine, scotch (neat, please), and cider. Seattle is my home, and I share an old house with my husband and cats.

I'm on my fourth—fifth?—rewatching of the modern *Doctor Who*, and I think one particular quote from that show sums up my entire life.

"We're all stories, in the end. Make it a good one, eh?" — *The Eleventh Doctor, Doctor Who*

I hope your story is brilliant.

You can reach me all over the web...
patriciadeddy.com
patricia@patriciadeddy.com

facebook.com/patriciadeddyauthor

twitter.com/patriciadeddy

instagram.com/patriciadeddy

bookbub.com/profile/patricia-d-eddy

amazon.com/author/pdeddy

ALSO BY PATRICIA D. EDDY

Away From Keyboard

Dive into a steamy mix of geekery and military prowess with the men and women of Hidden Agenda and Second Sight.

Breaking His Code

In Her Sights

On His Six

Second Sight

By Lethal Force

Fighting For Valor

Finding Their Forevers (a holiday short story)

Call Sign: Redemption

Midnight Coven

These novellas will take you into the darker side of the paranormal with vampires, witches, and more.

Forever Kept

Immortal Hunter

Wicked Omens

Twisted Captive

Elemental Shifter

Hot werewolves and strong, powerful elementals. What's not to love? The final two books in this series will be released at the end of 2020.

A Shift in the Water

A Shift in the Air

***

By the Fates

Check out the COMPLETE By the Fates series if you love dark and steamy tales of witches, devils, and an epic battle between good and evil.

By the Fates, Freed

Destined: A By the Fates Story

By the Fates, Fought

By the Fates, Fulfilled

***

In Blood

If you love hot Italian vampires and and a human who can hold her own against beings far stronger, then the In Blood series is for you.

Secrets in Blood

Revelations in Blood

Holidays and Heroes

Beauty isn't only skin deep and not all scars heal. Come swoon over sexy vets and the men and women who love them.

Mistletoe and Mochas

Love and Libations

Restrained

Do you like to be tied up? Or read about characters who do? Enjoy a fresh BDSM series that will leave you begging for more. Binge the completed series now!

In His Silks

Christmas Silks

All Tied Up For New Year's

In His Collar